Iqbal

A NOVEL

Written by
FRANCESCO D'ADAMO

Translated by
Ann Leonori

Simon & Schuster, London

First published in Great Britain by Simon & Schuster UK Ltd, 2004
A Viacom company

First published in the USA in 2003 by Atheneum Books
for Young Readers, an imprint of Simon & Schuster
Children's Publishing Division, New York.

Copyright © Edizioni EL, 2001
English language translation copyright © 2003 by Ann Leonori
First published in Italian in 2001 as *Storia di Iqbal* by Edizioni EL

1 3 5 7 9 10 8 6 4 2

Simon & Schuster UK Ltd
Africa House
64–78 Kingsway
London WC2B 6AH

A CIP catalogue record for this book is available from
the British Library

ISBN 0689837682

Printed and bound in Great Britain by
WS Bookwell, Finland

For Annarita

Introduction

All over the world and throughout history, children have been a source of labour. They have always had their share of work. In homes or in fields, they have contributed to the survival of their families or to the good of the community. In countries moving from agriculture to manufacturing, child labour is considered essential to successful development, and children have been present in virtually every field, workshop, and factory.

Today, more than two hundred million children between the ages of five and seventeen are "economically active" in the world. About seventy-three million of these are under ten years of age, and almost six million children are working in conditions of "forced and bonded labour." Bonded labour is a system in which a person works for a preestablished period of time to pay off a debt. Many of America's early colonists started out as indentured servants, receiving their passage to the colonies in return for a number of years of labour, after which they acquired their liberty and a grant of land.

In many countries, bonded child labour is considered an indispensable part of the economic system. When families are in debt, they "rent," or bond, their children, who can be as young as four or five, to work for "masters," who have complete control over the children's lives until the debt is paid, and who can even send the children on to other masters. In Pakistan, where *Iqbal* takes place, industries such as brick-making and carpet-making depend on child labour. The brick-making industry employs whole families, small children working alongside their parents in dangerous conditions.

Carpet-making is particularly dependent on children and their manual dexterity: small fingers can be taught to work quickly to tie the thousands of knots necessary to make a carpet. Working conditions are usually very poor. The children, often underfed, work from dawn to dusk, squatting for long hours on low benches in front of their looms, breathing dust and lint. Many of them are chained to their looms. There is no time for play and little time for rest. They are invisible to the outside world.

Iqbal is a fictional account about a real person, Iqbal Masih, and his crusade to liberate bonded labourers. The narrator is a young girl, Fatima, whose life was forever changed by his courage.

One

'Yes, I knew Iqbal. I think about him often. I like to. I feel I owe it to him. You see, for Iqbal I was not invisible. I existed, and he made me free. So here is his story. As I remember it. As I knew him.'

The house of our master, Hussain Khan, was in the outskirts of Lahore, not far from the dusty, dry countryside where flocks of sheep from the north grazed.

It was a big house, half stone, half sheet iron, facing a dirty courtyard containing a well, an old Toyota van, and a canopy of reeds that protected the bales of cotton and wool. Across the courtyard from the house was a long building, the carpet factory, where fourteen of us worked. We had all been bonded to Hussain Khan to pay off debts our families had contracted with local moneylenders. The building had a tin roof and a dirt floor, so it was hot in the summer and cold in the winter.

In the corner at the back of the courtyard, half-hidden by thorn bushes and weeds, you could just see a rusty iron door. Behind the door was a short, steep stairway that led down to the Tomb.

Work began half an hour before dawn, when the master's wife, dressed in her bathrobe and slippers, crossed the courtyard in the uncertain light of the fading night and brought us a round loaf of chapati bread and some dal, lentil soup. We all ate together, greedily dipping our bread into the large bowl on the ground, while we chatted incessantly of the dreams we had had during the night.

My grandmother and my mother used to say that dreams come from an unknown area of heaven, far far away, and they descend to earth when men call them. They can bring pain or comfort, joy or desperation, or sometimes they have no meaning and bring nothing. But it's not necessarily true that only bad men receive evil dreams and silly men empty ones. Who are we, after all, to understand the ways of heaven? What's really bad, my grandmother would say, is to receive *no* dreams. It's like not receiving the warmth of someone who is thinking of us even if they are far away.

I hadn't dreamed for months. I suspect many of us had stopped dreaming, but we were afraid to admit it: We felt so alone in the mornings. So we invented them, and they were always lovely dreams, full of light and colour and memories of home. We competed to see who could invent the most fantastic ones, speaking very fast with full mouths, until the mistress said, 'Enough already! Enough!'

Then we were allowed to pass – one by one – behind the filthy curtain that hid the Turkish toilet at the back of the big room where our looms and benches stood in rows. The first ones to go were those who had slept chained by their ankles to their looms. The master called them numskulls, because they worked slowly and poorly. They got the coloured yarns mixed up or made mistakes in the pattern (the worst possible error), or they cried too loudly over the blisters on their fingers.

The numskulls weren't very bright. Everybody else knew that all you had to do is take the knife we used for working and cut open the blister. The liquid drips out and it hurts for a while, but in time the skin grows back tougher, so you don't feel anything anymore. You just have to know how to bear the wait. Those of us who weren't chained sometimes felt sorry for the numskulls, but sometimes we teased them. Usually they were the new workers, just arrived, who hadn't learned that the only way we could become free was to work very hard and very fast, to erase each and every line on our small slates, until there were none left and we could return home.

Like the others, I had my own little slate hanging above the loom I worked on.

The day I arrived, many years before, Hussain Khan had taken a clean slate and had made some signs on it. 'This is your name.'

'Yes, sir.'

'This is your slate. Nobody can touch it. Do you understand?'

'Yes, sir.'

Then he drew many other lines, one next to the other, as straight as the hair on the back of a frightened dog, and every group of four had a line through it.

'Can you count?' the master asked.

'Almost up to ten,' I responded.

'Look,' Hussain Khan said, 'this is your debt. Every line is a rupee. I'll give you a rupee for every day you work. That's fair. Nobody would pay you more. Ask anyone you want: Everyone will say that Hussain Khan is a good and fair master who gives you what you deserve. And every day at sunset, I'll erase one of these lines, right in front of your eyes. You'll feel proud, and your parents will feel proud, because it will be the fruit of your work. Do you understand?'

'Yes, sir,' I answered again, but it wasn't true. I hadn't understood. I studied those mysterious lines, thick as trees in a forest, but I couldn't distinguish my name from the debt. It was as though they were the same thing.

'When all the lines are erased,' Hussain Khan added, 'when you see this slate wiped completely

4

clean, then you'll be free and you'll be able to return home.'

I never saw a clean slate, neither mine nor one of my companions'.

After the numskulls returned from the toilet behind the curtain and were chained to their looms, the rest of us were free to use the toilet and to splash some water on our faces. There was a small window high up in the wall, and through it you could see the open sky and just barely glimpse the branches of a flowering almond tree. Every morning I stayed an extra minute and tried desperately to grasp the old wooden frame and to pull myself up so that I could look outside. I was ten years old then, small and delicate as I still am, and I never even managed to touch the edge of the window. And yet, every day I felt that I had reached a little bit higher – perhaps a 'nothing,' only a fraction of an inch – but I was sure that soon I would be able to hoist myself up and lean out just far enough to touch the bark of the almond tree through the open air.

Of course, if I ever did manage to reach through the window or even to wriggle out, I would just find myself in the garden next door and Hussain Khan's wife would come to get me, brandishing her stick and crying, 'You, little ragbag! You ungrateful little viper!' I would end up in the Tomb for at least three days, perhaps for more. That's what would probably happen.

But still, every morning I tried.

I had been working for Hussain Khan for three years, and I had never been put in the Tomb. Some of the other children were envious, and said I was Hussain Khan's pet and that's why he didn't punish me. It wasn't true. I was never punished because I worked quickly and well. I ate what they gave me without complaint, and when the master was around I kept silent, not like some, who answered back. I'll admit that sometimes the master *did* pat my head and say, 'Little Fatima, my little Fatima,' but all the while I trembled. I was frightened and wanted to disappear, to hide. Hussain Khan was fat, with a black beard and small eyes. His hands were oily from palm oil and left a greasy mark on whatever he touched.

Some nights, when I was still able to dream, I imagined Hussain Khan sneaking up in the dark to where I slept next to the loom. I could hear his heavy breathing and the smell of smoke on his jacket; I could hear the sound of his feet on the dusty earth. He would caress me, saying, 'Little Fatima.' The next morning, hidden behind the dirty curtain at the back of the room, I would examine my body to see if there were signs of oil. There were none. It was only a nightmare.

Work began at sunrise. The mistress clapped her hands three times and we all sat down at our looms. After a moment we began to work rhythmically, tying the knots, beating them down. While we were working we were forbidden to stop, to talk, or to let our minds wander. We could only stare at the countless coloured threads, from which we had to choose the right one to insert into the carpet pattern. The master had assigned each of us a pattern.

As the morning passed, the air filled with heat, dust, and flying lint, and the sound of the looms slipped into the voice of the awakening city. The motors of old cars and loaded trucks, the braying of the donkeys, the shouts of men, and the cries of the vendors in the nearby market – all these grew louder as the day came to life, as Lahore came out into the streets. When my arms and shoulders started aching, I would briefly turn my head towards the door to the courtyard and sunlight, and I would guess how much time remained before my only pause of the day. My hands worked on their own, out of habit. They chose the threads, pulled the knots. Again and again. They passed the weft, beat it down with the comb, then started knotting. Again and again. That evening Hussain Khan would measure my work. He'd judge whether it was up to standards, if it was made carefully, and then he'd erase one of the lines on my slate – a rupee for a day's work.

He had been erasing those lines for three years, and they were still all there, or at least that's how it seemed to me. Sometimes I even thought there were more of them, but that wasn't possible – the lines on the slate couldn't be like the weeds in my father's garden that grew overnight and crowded the crops.

When we finally stopped for lunch we were dulled by fatigue. We dragged ourselves out into the courtyard and sat in the sun around the well to eat our chapati and vegetables and drink water, because our throats were dry and full of lint. Very few of us had enough energy to talk or laugh. Our break lasted an hour, but our hunger a good deal longer. Then we went back into the workroom, while Hussain Khan and his wife retired into their house to escape the heat of the afternoon. For a few hours there was no need to supervise us. Nobody had the courage to run away and anyway we couldn't *not* work. In the evening the master's measuring tape would reveal to the last centimetre how we had spent our time.

Not enough work done, no rupee, no line erased from our slates; we knew it well.

This was my life for three years. The first months I thought a lot about my family – my mother, my brothers and sisters – our home, the countryside, the buffalo that pulled the plow, the sweet *laddu* my mother made with chickpea flour, the desserts and almonds that we ate on feast days. But as time went on these memories faded like old, worn carpets.

That is, until the day Iqbal arrived.

Two

Iqbal appeared one morning just as summer was about to begin. The sun was high and warm, and its long beams of light caught the eddying dust in the workroom. Two beams crossed right in the middle of my carpet, accentuating the bright colours, and I imagined they were swords clashing in a mortal duel. One was the sword of the good hero; the other was of an evil villian. My hands, as they made knots, could give the hero's sword a slight advantage, moving the other sword away for a brief second, but the implacable evil sword returned.

One of the boys, Karim, said he had been to the cinema twice, and that the movies told stories of good and evil. After great tribulation, the hero always triumphed. Then he put on a beautiful suit of coloured silk and asked for the hand of his favourite maiden. The father couldn't refuse. No, he was happy, because the hero had risked his life. Good had defeated evil. Karim, who was almost seventeen and whose fingers had grown too thick and awkward to make the thin, delicate knots of the carpets, had become a sort of overseer to us children. It was probably true that he had been to the movies even if such luck seemed incredible to us because some evenings when he was in a good mood, Karim told us the movie stories with all their details, and he couldn't have invented them. He didn't have enough imagination. They were long, complicated films. It took him two months to tell us the story of the first one. When we reached the end, we couldn't remember the beginning and we asked him to start all over. I thought I'd like to go to the cinema someday. My father and mother had never been, nor my brothers and sisters. They were too poor. The cinema was a luxury for city folks. Like television.

The master and the mistress had a television. Sometimes at night, when we were trying to fall asleep, we could hear those strange voices in Hussain Khan's living room and see the coloured lights through the rush matting at the window. Karim, always Karim, bragged that once he had sneaked up to one of the windows, and had seen almost five minutes of a cricket game.

'What's cricket?' I asked.

'Shut up, stupid!' he answered.

If you want my opinion, though, it was a big lie. It's true that Karim did everything the master wanted and that he supervised us, because otherwise he would have had nowhere to go and nothing to eat, but he would never have had the courage to peek into the master's windows. It was big trouble for anyone to go near the house.

Suddenly I realised that I had to get back to work. My mind had wandered. Just in time I managed to recapture a thread I was about to lose. Then the sunbeams were blocked and the two swords of light stopped fighting. We all turned around to see the master standing in the doorway. His big body filled it. He was dressed for travelling, with a long coat that almost reached his feet and boots covered with red dust. In his left hand he held a sack, and his right hand held the arm of a boy in an iron grip. The boy was thin and dark and not very tall; he looked about two years older than me.

My first impression was that he was handsome. Then I thought, *No, he isn't really good-looking.* But he had such eyes. They were sweet and deep and they weren't afraid. He was standing at the threshold of the workroom with Hussain Khan's enormous hand gripping his arm and we were all looking at him. The fourteen of us child-slaves plus Karim, all observing another slave. He was one of the many who had come and gone over the years, but we felt that somehow, *this* new boy was different. He looked around at us, one by one. He was sad, of course, like anyone who has been away from home for a long time, like anyone who is little more than a slave, like anyone who can't imagine what will become of him.

But I'm telling you this: He wasn't afraid.

Hussain Khan looked at us and growled, 'What do you think you're looking at? Get back to work.'

We bent to our looms, but then we quickly peeked over our shoulders. Hussain brought the new boy over to an empty loom in the row next to mine, pulled out a rusty shackle, and locked it on the boy's right ankle.

'This will be your place, here's where you'll work,' he said. 'And if you work well—'

'I know,' the boy responded.

Hussain took the usual slate, already covered with lines.

'This is your debt,' he began, 'and every evening I—'

'I know,' said the new boy.

'Alright, then,' said Hussain, 'alright, Mister Know-it-all. Your old master told me that you're stubborn and proud. He also told me, however, that nobody knows how to work like you, when you want to. . . . We'll see. We'll see.'

Hussain headed towards the door. Once there he stopped and pointed his fat finger towards Karim.

'And you, keep an eye on him!'

Karim nodded uncertainly.

The new boy sat at his loom and began to work. We watched him in silence, our mouths open. Nobody was as fast and skillful as he, nobody knew how to tighten the knots with such precision and delicacy. His fingers flew, even though the pattern Hussain had assigned him was one of the most difficult.

One thing was for certain: He wasn't chained because he was a numskull. Oh, no. It was for some other reason.

'What's your name?' asked Karim, trying to make his voice sound tough.

'Iqbal,' he answered. 'Iqbal Masih.'

Three

That same night, as soon as the master had turned out the lights and we felt sure that he was asleep, little Al` went to guard the door while a few of us crept along to meet the new boy. Karim came, too. Although he could never forget his responsibilities as overseer, his curiosity had got the best of him. Salman, a boy of ten who seemed older because he was so hard and tough, came too. The skin of his face and hands was pitted by three years' work in a brick factory near Karachi. Maria also wanted to meet the new boy. She was a little girl, younger than me and tiny as a bird. She had arrived at the beginning of the winter, but nobody had yet heard her say a word. We didn't know if she was a mute. We gave her her name. She had learned it immediately. She slept curled up like a small animal near her loom and she followed me everywhere like a shadow.

Iqbal was awake. We could hear his chain rattle in the darkness. You could never sleep the first night in a new place. You felt lonely and you wanted to talk. All of us understood that. Most of us had had two or three masters, some even more. So we settled down near him. It was a moonless night and we could barely see.

'Be careful, Ali,' we said. The master had got very angry when he'd last caught us awake at night. He said that it always made us stupid and slow the next day.

Ali answered with a series of short whistles that meant 'Coast clear.'

We whispered some questions and waited to hear Iqbal's story.

Iqbal began, 'My father used to go out early in the morning, when the first rays of sun appeared, and harness our buffalo to the light plow. At that hour, even in summer, the air was still fresh and pleasant. All around we could see the cultivated fields and the other peasants, starting the day in the same way. I'd go with him, carrying the bottle of water and the vegetables my mother had fixed for him. At first my father would work easily and his thin arms wouldn't seem to feel the effort, but after a couple of hours he'd have to slow down. The earth was like stone. The sweat ran down his face and chest, and the red dust covered his hair. The plow didn't dig like before, and even the buffalo lowed from the heat. Between midday and three the sun beat

15

down mercilessly, and it was too hot to work. The boundaries of our world seemed to disappear in the haze. So we lay in the shade of a tree, eating and drinking water, while the buffalo twitched his tail nervously to keep the insects away. 'This is a blessed land,' my father would say, 'it's good and fertile, well irrigated. Look how everything grows. All you have to do is throw down a seed and by the grace of God a family could live forever in abundance. Remember that, Iqbal.'

'Yes, Father,' I would answer. But there was never abundance in our house. There was never enough food and my older brother was often ill. Once I asked my father why this was so. Why were all the wheat and oats and vegetables that we cultivated loaded onto carts the same day they were picked? Why in our hut was there only a sack of broken grain and another of dried chickpeas next to the fireplace? 'Because all this belongs to the master,' my father had replied.

'And that's right?'

'He's the master,' said my father. 'Who are we?"

'My father always said the same thing,' interrupted Salman, 'but then he also said that the master was greedy and evil. In the privacy of our home he would curse the master terribly. My mother would shiver and beg him, 'Stop, please! If he ever heard you . . .' She was convinced that the master had a thousand eyes and ears. Women!' Salman concluded, 'they don't understand anything.'

I would have liked to tell Salman what I thought. Maybe, in his opinion, we girls were stupid and useless. But I know I worked as hard as he did, some days even more. Still, I held my peace, because Salman was difficult. He was a rebel. He had been down in the Tomb once for two days, and when he emerged, parched from the heat and stung by the scorpions, he just spat in the dirt.

To him, nothing was as bad as working at the brick-kiln. But he had always refused to tell us what brick-making was like. I couldn't even begin to imagine it, but I prayed that the master would never sell me to the owner of a brick factory.

'It's wrong to curse our masters,' declared Karim. 'What would we do without Hussain Khan? He's the one who feeds us and protects us. He lets us work so that we can pay off our family's debt.'

'Yeah,' jeered Salman, 'and he's the one who will kick you out one of these days when you're no longer any use to him. You'll end up hungry and alone, wandering in the streets.'

'That's not so,' protested Karim. 'The master knows that I'm loyal and he needs me.'

'Right, to spy on us.'

I thought they were going to start fighting right there in the dark. Salman was right: Karim was always ready to tell Hussain Khan everything that happened in the workshop. But then sometimes it seemed that

Karim was on our side. I couldn't understand it.

'My father's a good man,' continued Iqbal. 'He's never cursed anyone. He's always accepted his destiny. Even when my brother got worse and coughed all night every night, my father didn't curse anyone. He called the doctor from the village, and the doctor came with his bag and his glasses. He bent down over the bed and used an instrument to listen to the inside of my brother. First inside his chest, then inside his back, and he shook his head.'

'I know,' said Karim. 'I've seen it done, too.'

'Then he talked to my father, took his hat and the bamboo cane, and left. My mother was crying. She had already lost other children. The next morning, while we were harnessing the buffalo to the plow, my father told me that the doctor would return with medicine that might save my brother. And the doctor did return, and there was another man with him, well dressed, a merchant or landowner, and he spoke to my father, too. At a certain point he pulled some money out of a belt he had round his waist and showed it to my father, who only said, "No."'

'And what happened to your brother?' I asked.

'He didn't get better. My father didn't have anyone who could help him in the fields; I was too young and weak then. He talked to my mother for a long time. Then he rode the buffalo to the village. He came back when it was getting on towards evening and went out to hoe the fields without even changing his clothes, and when it got dark, he came in, breathing heavily. He didn't even eat dinner, but called me over and told me that a man would lend him a large sum of money, 'Twenty-six dollars,' he said. I tried to figure it out in rupees but couldn't. With that money the family would be able to survive until the next harvest, and my brother would receive more medicine and God willing, get well. He said I would have to work to help the family pay off the debt, and we wouldn't meet for many months, but I would learn how to make carpets and this might help me in life.'

'My father had a debt, too,' I whispered in the dark, 'after the embankment broke and he lost everything. A man came to talk to him, and then Hussain came and brought me here.'

Iqbal continued, 'My father said that he could send one of my sisters, but I said, 'No, send me.' He hugged me and asked if I was afraid. 'No,' I said, but I was lying. The carpet maker came the next morning. He came by car, and was very nice, even to my mother. 'I'm taking you to the city,' he said. 'You'll like it, just wait and see.' I looked through the rear window of the car, and the last thing I saw while he took me away was my father whipping the poor buffalo, pushing it through the field. You should have heard the poor beast lowing.'

'Oh, well,' said Karim, 'it won't take you long to

pay off your father's debt. I know – I've seen a lot. Nobody works as fast or as well as you do. You'll erase those lines on the slate like the sun erases the snow on the mountains.'

In the dark I saw Iqbal's teeth flash briefly, as if he had smiled.

'The debt is never erased,' he said softly. 'It doesn't matter how good you are.'

'You're crazy!' cried Salman. 'You're saying those things because you're mean. You're trying to frighten us. Every day the master erases a line, and once he's finished, we'll go home. It was like that with the bricks, too, believe me. We had to make a thousand bricks a day and we got one hundred rupees for every thousand. All my family worked there. Even my sister.'

'And did you cancel your debt?' asked Iqbal.

'No,' grunted Salman, 'but what does that mean? Some days it was too rainy. Sometimes the clay was too sandy. Sometimes the bricks broke when they came out of the kiln, and then just bad luck . . .'

'Have you ever seen anyone pay off their debt?' asked the new boy.

In the dark I could feel Maria hugging herself close to me. Who knew if she could hear and understand what we were saying? I understood too well, and it annoyed me that *that* boy, the newcomer, dared to say such things. I wanted to scream, 'You're wrong! You liar!' but even though I barely knew him, he didn't seem like that kind of person.

'No,' we all said, one after the other, 'no, we've never seen anyone pay off their debt.'

Salman tried to get a word in. 'And yet—'

Ali, who was guarding the door, let out two shrill whistles. The alarm.

We all crept quickly back to our beds. I tried to fall asleep but couldn't. I kept turning this way and that. After a while I crawled back over the dusty dirt floor. The new boy, Iqbal, was still awake, too. I spoke in his ear, so the others wouldn't hear me.

'What do you mean,' I asked, 'by saying we'll never get away from here? We'll never go home?'

'Who are you?' he asked.

'My name's Fatima.'

There was silence for a few seconds.

'Can you keep a secret, Fatima?' he whispered.

'Of course I can. What do you take me for?'

'Then I can tell you,' he said, lowering his voice even more. 'We'll get away from here. You can bet on it.'

'You said it was impossible to pay off the debt.'

'It is, but that's not how we'll go.'

'How, then? I'm beginning to think that the master was right to call you a know-it-all.'

'We'll run away, that's what we'll do.'

'You're crazy!'

'I'm not. We'll run away. You'll come with me.'

I didn't know him. He could have been just a braggart, or maybe even truly crazy, but I still believed him. I went back to my bed and spent the night turning restlessly.

four

For more than a month after Iqbal's arrival nothing new happened. The heat got worse and worse, and we worked harder and harder. Hussain Khan moved nervously around the workshop, distributing threats and promises, oily caresses and slaps, all the while wringing his hands and invoking the name of Allah and the Prophet in vain.

We old-timers knew only too well that he was expecting a visit from clients, probably foreigners. Our master was worried that the carpets we were making wouldn't be beautiful or perfect enough to satisfy these illustrious customers. He tried endearments – *my little ones, little doves,* and even *my beloved children.* He reminded us that he had freed us from a life of hunger and hardship. He begged us not to ruin him – because his ruin would be ours. And then he threatened us with the most horrible punishments. And indeed, when clients were about to arrive, it was easy to end up in the Tomb for the slightest mistake.

When we stopped working at sunset we were exhausted. Our fingers bled from all the cuts the threads made. Karim was the one who feared Hussain Khan's anger the most. If he was kicked out, what could he do? With no home or family to go to, he'd end up alone in some corner of the *suk*.

So during the day, if we dared raise our heads for a second, we were victim to Karim's angry outbursts and his threats to tell on us. At night, however, he would take pity on our tears and our tortured hands. He would get up from his pallet and light a lamp, grumbling that we were all good-for-nothings, but then he'd give us some ointment for our wounds.

Even if many of us were punished because Karim told on us, I have to say that he wasn't so bad. We all knew his story: He had been sold to Hussain Khan when he was little more than seven, and since then Khan's house had become his house, too. I think that Karim was a little fond of Hussain Khan, even though he, too, had slaved and suffered like the rest of us. Now that he was so big and therefore useless for working on the loom, he was afraid he'd be thrown away like an old, outgrown pair of shoes.

We hated him when he got us punished, but we also understood that his destiny might be ours one day – though we didn't think much about the future.

The only one who remained untouched by Hussain's storm of threats was Iqbal. He was rarely corrected, and Hussain didn't try false, oily caresses, either. He usually just passed Iqbal's loom, checking on the work without saying anything. Iqbal ignored Hussain. He didn't let his attention wander from his work. He didn't cry. He didn't whine. He didn't even make faces or gestures behind Hussain's back.

'See? Chaining's tamed him,' sneered one of the boys.

'No, no,' said another, 'he wants to become the master's pet.'

I knew that these things weren't true. But Iqbal paid no attention to the comments. Since we shared the same fate and the same kind of life, you'd think we children would feel united, but instead we quarrelled and separated into little groups. The big ones always bullied the little ones – as though bullying could change our destiny or make us feel better.

'Just ignore them,' Iqbal would say.

One day, while we were trying to catch our breath during our lunch break in the courtyard, Karim started to put on mysterious airs like he was about to tell us some secret of the master's.

'We have to treat our new friend with respect,' he said, pointing to Iqbal. 'He's special. He's precious. I heard Hussain Khan say so to another carpet maker.'

We were all ears.

'And what's so special about him?'

Karim waited until he was sure he had everybody's concentrated attention. Then he looked around to make sure that Hussain or his wife couldn't hear, shrugged his shoulders, spat in the dust, lowered his voice, and whispered, 'The rug, the one he's weaving, isn't like all the others. No. It's a Blue Bukhara. Ever heard of them? Only two are made each year, maybe three. Hussain said so; I heard him with these very ears. A carpet like that is worth a lot of money, and not just anybody can make one. You need an artist for a carpet like that.'

Here he stopped, and spat in the dust again.

'Our friend here is an artist. Who would have ever thought it, eh?'

All eyes turned to Iqbal.

'Is that true?' we asked.

Iqbal was as red as a chili pepper.

'I don't know,' he muttered.

'Of course he knows,' Karim went on, 'he's already made one. Hussain said so. He said it.'

'Is it true? Is it true?' we asked again.

'I had three masters before Hussain Khan,' Iqbal answered, 'and yes, for one of them I made a carpet like that.'

'And how did you do it?'

'I don't know. I just copied the design they gave me.'

We sat there in silence for a few minutes.

'But . . . but if that's the case,' said a boy who came from India, 'then why did your other masters sell you?'

'I don't know,' Iqbal said in a low voice.

You could see he was embarrassed and he wasn't happy that Karim had revealed Hussain's secret.

'And you, Karim, you who know everything, do *you* know why his masters sold him, if he's as good as you say?'

'Of course I know, but I can't tell you. The master trusts me and doesn't like me to talk about his private matters.'

We all snickered at that excuse, and Karim got mad. Once we had calmed down again, a dark-skinned boy from the south who had seen the sea stood up from the edge of the well where he had been sitting.

'But then,' the boy said, 'then the master will erase your lines. If that carpet is worth so much, he'll cancel your debt.'

We all nodded. We had never seen such luck.

'You can be sure about it,' cried Karim. 'You should see how worried Hussain Khan is that Iqbal won't finish in time or that he won't do it well or that he'll make some mistake, and the rug will have to be thrown away. Oh, he'll cancel the debt all right. You all know how generous and fair our master is.'

Many of us had doubts about that, but we observed Iqbal with new envy. He was going to succeed.

'Hussain won't cancel the debt,' Iqbal said slowly. 'My other masters didn't. The debt is never cancelled.'

So what hope did we have? Why then did we work from dawn till dusk? What right did Iqbal have to claim such awful things? After all, he was the newest arrival and luckier than everybody else. How could he crush us like that?

Even Salman and Ali thought he was lying and that he would be freed.

'You're a liar!' shouted Ali, almost in tears.

Salman trembled with anger.

In the following days many of us started to resent Iqbal, saying that he was arrogant and that he sided with Karim and Hussain Khan.

I tried to defend him, but I was only a little girl.

I had fallen into the habit of sliding over to Iqbal's pallet and chatting with him almost every night before going to sleep. I didn't believe the mean talk about him, and if the master cancelled his debt, well, I'd be happy for him.

We would sit in the dark and listen to the city: the sound of the traffic that never stopped, but that at night became dulled and muffled; sudden voices; the mumbling of a man who hadn't respected the precept of no alcohol; and those mysterious, confused city night sounds that we couldn't identify. We had both been born in the countryside, and there the noises that broke the silence of the night all had a name and a familiar origin: a bird of prey, a buffalo roaming free, a stray dog wild on following a scent, and sometimes the rustle of a restless spirit whose mark we would find on the bark of a tree the following morning. We never really feared the spirits, because we understood they were a part of the natural world.

But we didn't know city life. We had only caught glimpses of it through van windows when the master took us away from our families and brought us to the carpet factory. I remembered people running from one place to another, more people than I had ever seen before, and they all looked like they didn't really know where they were going.

Iqbal could remember more about cities, because he had changed masters. Once he had seen dozens of kites dancing in the spring sky. And he remembered a bus – one of those enormous, shiny, multicoloured buses we have in Pakistan, full of headlights and tail-lights and chrome, with horns that blast like a whole herd of buffalo so that they can make their way through the chaos of traffic. It had been the first time he had seen one.

'Me?' said Iqbal. 'I'd like to get on one of those buses and sit down next to a window and go all around the city – twice, even – to see where all those people are running to.'

'No, no,' I said, 'it'd be more fun to go to the cinema and see one of those love stories Karim tells us about. There are even big, bright posters with the stories and pictures of the actors all over the city. Some of them are so famous that people recognise them on the street.'

'Actors don't walk around in the streets.'

'What do you know about it? Some do.'

Sometimes we talked about our families, what we still recalled about them, or even what we had already forgotten and would never remember again. I had no recollection of my father, and only a faded image of my mother, but Iqbal could remember everything. He remembered his relatives and his village. He even remembered exactly where things were placed in the hut he lived in. He described to me how his father always got up before dawn to go down to the stream to wash, and then walked towards the stable with his hair still wet.

Iqbal confessed that he went over his memories, one by one, every night before he went to sleep, so he wouldn't forget them.

'What do you do with them?' I asked.

'They help me,' he answered.

'To do what?'

'To get away from here.'

I didn't want to embarrass him, so I didn't mention the idea of escaping to him again. I thought he had said it to impress me or that maybe it made him feel better to pretend it was possible.

There's nothing wrong with Iqbal believing we'll be free someday, I thought.

And I also thought, *If only we could!*

But to escape meant having a place to escape to, and what could I do, outside in a city I didn't know and that frightened me? Who would protect me from all those noises I couldn't even name? I'd probably end up like Karim, who preferred to stay with Hussain Khan. But still, I'd never tell on Iqbal's plans.

Maybe that was why I could never reach the edge of the bathroom window frame: I was afraid of what lay beyond.

And why should someone like Iqbal – someone who was about to be freed after paying his debt – why should he want to run away? It didn't make sense to me.

So I kept my peace.

But three days later, just as the foreign buyers were about to arrive, Iqbal didn't keep his.

five

It was a special morning. When foreign customers arrived, Hussain Khan couldn't bully us too badly in their presence. He had to convince them that we were treated well.

'These are my apprentices,' he would say, distributing affectionate pats left and right. 'Here they learn an honest profession that will assure them a better future, one without hunger and poverty. They're like my own family.'

I really don't know if the foreigners believed him or not. Foreigners were funny that way. You didn't know what to make of them. Usually they were elegantly dressed men with cold eyes, but every now and then a woman would visit, a lady whose legs and arms weren't covered, and she would say, 'What lovely children!'

I'm not so sure we were so lovely.

That morning we had a bigger breakfast than usual – which alone put us in a good mood – and we were allowed to laugh and chat while we waited to pass the filthy curtain outside the bathroom.

The numskulls had already finished, and for the sake of the foreigners they wouldn't be chained to their looms that day. The rest of us were waiting on line, pushing and shoving.

'Be good, children! Be good,' called the mistress, but it didn't sound like her usual nasty warning. Even Hussain, who usually appeared halfway through the morning pulling up his trousers and sleepy-eyed, was already awake and agitated. He was sweaty and talked nonstop.

Karim was terrified by the idea that something could go wrong and that Hussain would blame it on him. The finished carpets were ready in the storage room and the ones in making were on display on the looms. There was almost a festive air to the place. I was waiting for my turn, little Maria hanging on to my skirt, and I was trying to avoid Ali's elbows and Salman's pinches. I felt a strange feeling inside me, one like wind in my breast. I was sure that I could jump very high – soar and finally reach the edge of that window frame.

Certainly nobody could have imagined what was going to happen.

Nobody was paying much attention to Iqbal, who

was standing beside his loom. Most of the children avoided him, because they were envious. Also he tended to keep to himself, as though he was occupied with serious thoughts.

I never got my turn at the bathroom that morning, and I never reached the window that looked out on the flowering almond.

Hussain, nervous and excited, paced around the workshop. Suddenly he stopped and turned white. He was looking at something behind us. I remember his shocked eyes and his mouth slowly opening and revealing his tobacco-blackened teeth. I'll never forget what I saw next.

Iqbal was standing next to his loom. Behind him was his carpet, that marvellous carpet with its complicated design in a rich blue that had never been seen before. It was perfect. Iqbal had worked better and faster than anyone else could have. The foreigners would go crazy over a rug like that.

Iqbal was pale, too, but not as pale as Hussain Khan. He took the knife that we all used to cut the ends of the knots, raised it above his head, and seemed to look each of us in the eye. Then he calmly turned and cut the carpet from top to bottom, right through the middle.

No, I thought, *don't . . . !*

In the silence that had fallen over the workshop we heard the distinct *rrrriipp* of the sliced threads.

Hussain Khan screamed like a stuck pig. The mistress screamed. Karim screamed, because he always did everything they did. We saw them take off across the room, raising a cloud of dust and lint, tripping over each other, cursing and swearing as true believers should never do.

Before they could grab him and take the knife away, Iqbal had cut twice more and the world's most beautiful blue carpet was in pieces on the red earth of the floor.

The silence seemed to last forever. Instinctively looking for protection, we had gathered in a corner of the workshop. Hussain Khan was standing in front of Iqbal, threatening Iqbal with his sheer size. His face was red and the swollen veins in his neck looked ready to burst. He was holding the knife he had taken from Iqbal and for a terrible moment we all thought, *He's going to kill him!*

The mistress sobbed and collected the pieces of rug from the floor, wiping off the red dust as if a miracle might put them back together.

Karim held his head in his hands. He was desperate, even though it wasn't his property.

'Hell child!' hissed Hussain. 'Hell child! They said you were a rebel, a traitor. They said, 'Hussain, don't trust him! He's a viper. A poisonous snake. An ingrate.' But I, blind and stupid, I thought . . . you'll pay for this, oh, you'll pay.'

'Into the Tomb,' howled the mistress, 'throw him in the Tomb and never let him out again!'

They grabbed him by the arms and dragged him into the courtyard. We followed, but stopped at the door like a group of frightened baby chicks. We saw Iqbal's knees scrape on the stones on the ground, his arm bang against the edge of the well. The master stopped at the rusty iron door and pulled it slowly open on rasping hinges. We saw him disappear down the steps into the dark, jerking Iqbal after him. Then we heard the awful, terrifying sound that haunted our sleep: the grate of the Tomb as it was raised and then *bang!* as it fell closed. The sound echoed in the heavy heat of the courtyard.

We couldn't breathe. The air was motionless. The dust lay still. Only the horseflies stirred, continuing to bite at our legs, but nobody even attempted to swat them away.

Hussain Khan came back up from underground. We heard his slow heavy footsteps. When he emerged into the sun he squinted his eyes. He closed the door with one final push and approached us where we were still clinging together at the entrance to the workshop.

'To work!' he growled.

We returned to our looms. We took up our work. All together. The same movements. The same sound of the comb.

Tunf. Tunf. Tunf.

Hussain stood behind us, in silence. We could feel his eyes look through us.

Tunf. Tunf. Tunf.

Ali, who worked on my right, mouthed the words, 'Why did he do it?'

I gestured quickly, 'I don't know.'

As he was being dragged over the stones of the courtyard, just a second before he disappeared, Iqbal had turned his head and looked at me. He wanted to say something.

I wasn't sure I understood. But one thing seemed clear: Iqbal was as frightened as we were, but he had done it, all the same.

Six

The Tomb was an old cistern, buried under the courtyard, closed by a grating at the foot of a damp, slippery stairway leading up to the iron door. There was no light down there, according to those who had been locked in, except around mid-afternoon, when a few rays of sunshine managed to filter through the holes and cracks caused by age and rust in the door to the courtyard. And there was virtually no air: You nearly suffocated down there.

'You can't breathe,' said Salman, who had experienced the Tomb a few months before because he had accidentally broken the blue-and-gold-flowered glazed pitcher the mistress used when she brought us water in the morning.

'You feel yourself suffocating and you think you're going to go mad. It feels like someone's grabbing your throat and squeezing. And then there's the dark. After a while you begin to see strange shapes, and colours, too, but they don't help you; they only scare you. I heard of someone who went crazy in the Tomb and nobody recognised him.'

'And then there are spiders,' another boy said, a boy who came from the mountains and talked differently, 'this big,' and he showed the palm of his hand. 'And scorpions: They're bad. They pinch and sting and they're poisonous. And then there are snakes.'

'There aren't any snakes,' Salman said scornfully. 'There's no water anymore.'

'Yes there are,' answered the mountain boy. 'I saw them.'

'You've never been in the Tomb.' Salman silenced him. 'You'd better keep quiet.'

That night we were all wide-awake, despite our fatigue and hunger. The master had made us work an extra hour after sunset and hadn't given us any dinner. The foreign clients had come, they had barely noticed us, they had loaded the carpets into their vans and cars, and they had left. Probably Hussain Khan had done good business. Usually after the departure of foreigners he celebrated with the mistress late into the night and we could hear music playing from the radio. But it wasn't our music, the music we heard at fairs when the men gathered to sell their animals. The master played a strange, noisy music, and we couldn't understand the words of the songs.

'Foreign stuff,' Karim said knowingly, 'music that comes from far away.'

But after this visit by the foreigners the house was dark and silent, menacing.

'You'll all pay,' Hussain had said before he went to bed, 'you'll pay for your friend. Because you were all in on it, I'm positive.'

Only a couple of the dim-witted and timorous children had tried to claim that they had no part in Iqbal's rebellion. But they had been pinched into silence. Who of us could be mad at Iqbal? We were all too worried.

'It's too hot,' I said. 'How can he survive down there?'

'It'll be like the brick-kiln,' said Salman, 'maybe worse. I can't remember anyone being put in the Tomb in midsummer. Can you?'

Everybody shook their heads. The sun had been unforgiving that afternoon, and we were covered in sweat, even now that it was night, and we could feel our heads boil, like in a fever.

Please, just shut up! Just shut up! I wanted to scream. Maria and Ali shook with fear at my side.

'I saw someone come out of the Tomb in summer,' said Karim, in his deep, almost grown-up voice. 'Five days Hussain kept him there. It happened many years ago. I was little then, but I can remember well. There was this boy, bigger than me; I don't know where he came from. One of his ears was missing, and he had a fierce look. He was like a wild dog, and we were afraid of him.'

'What did he do?' we asked.

'He refused to work, that's what. So Hussain whipped him. He whipped him good – you should have seen it. The boy didn't make a sound.'

'And then?'

'He kept on refusing to work. And when Hussain got near him with the whip again, ready to skin him alive, you know what he did? He bit into Hussain's arm and wouldn't let go.' Karim spat in the dust. 'Just like a dog.'

'So the master put him in the Tomb?'

'Five days he kept him there.'

'And did he come out?'

'Yeah, he came out. They carried him out like the dead, but he didn't die. He was all burned from the heat and his skin had peeled away. He lay for a week on his pallet, and we put a wet rag on his face. Then he got up and began to work. Anyway, he was never the same. He was still like a dog, but like the kind that carries his tail between his legs.'

'Iqbal won't be like that,' I exclaimed.

'He'll give in, too,' said Karim. 'What do you think? He's not so special. Probably he's defied all the masters he's had, and that's why they keep selling him, even though he's so skilled. But Hussain, he

41

knows what to do with him.'

'Iqbal won't give in,' I repeated, 'and we have to help him.'

There were a few vague murmurs of agreement.

'Help him?' muttered Karim. 'So far we've skipped dinner thanks to him.'

'You can just shut up – you ate anyway,' Salman answered back. 'I saved some bread.'

'And I have some water,' I said. 'Let's go.'

'You're crazy,' yelled Karim, 'I forbid you . . . If the master finds out he'll take it out on me.'

'Shut up!' Salman repeated.

We slipped towards the door of the workshop, which Hussain Khan triple-locked every night – a useless precaution, in my opinion. After all, where could we go?

'He has the keys,' said Salman, and he pointed to Karim. 'Open it. Fast.'

'Forget it!'

'Let's do it this way. You open the door and you come along. If the master finds out, you can say we were trying to escape and that you were coming after us to catch us. But if you don't help, I swear . . .'

It's true that Karim was older, but he was thin and weak and had never been very brave, while Salman was strong as an ox and feared by all.

Karim scratched his head, stood on one foot, then on the other, and looked around for moral support.

Not finding any, he spat in the dirt – angry and frustrated.

He found the big iron keys deep in the folds of his trousers, sniffed a bit, acted the victim a little longer, then opened the door.

It was just past midnight when we found ourselves outside. It was a moonless night, with a clean, black sky, because there are rarely clouds in the sky on a summer night. The air barely moved the leaves in the trees. We stood in the doorway for a minute, so our sweaty faces could dry.

I wonder what it's like down there, I asked myself, and I shivered with fear.

Stubborn little Ali followed us, and we crawled to the edge of the well. The master's house seemed dark and forbidding. We knew that Hussain Khan slept like an ox. Some nights his snoring sounded like a thunderstorm, but the mistress . . . *she* heard every sound, the slightest rustling, even, I bet, the wing beat of a night bird. We had often seen her in her bathrobe, wandering around in the dark, muttering fiercely as she pried into every corner of the courtyard.

'And what if they see us?'

From the edge of the well two leaps would take us to the safety of Hussain's van. It smelled of gas and burnt oil. From there, however, the way to the iron door that led to the Tomb offered no hiding places, but passed right below one of Hussain's bedroom windows. I was afraid it would be impossible to sneak by without waking the mistress. She was standing there – I was positive – hidden behind the curtains like a predatory animal, waiting for us to take just one step.

For a second I thought it would be better to go back, but then I felt ashamed. I turned to look at Salman: He was probably afraid, too, but he knew he had to try first. After all, I was only a girl, right? And Al` was too little.

He swallowed hard, then whispered, 'Here I go.'

He began to crawl on his elbows and knees, holding the packet of bread in his teeth. He went slowly, his rear end pointed up to the sky so that it seemed anyone could spot him slinking about . . . He continued to shift pebbles, and seemed to be making such noise – and then suddenly he disappeared into the shadows. In the few moments of silence between one snore and another, we heard a couple of noises and then a short hiss.

'Go!' I said to Ali.

He ran as lightly as a kitten. He was gone in a second.

Another hiss.

Well, I said to myself, *now it's your turn.*

I left cover. I had to crawl while holding the bottle of water, which threatened to spill at every movement.

I kept telling myself that it wasn't really very far from the van to the rusty door, just a few metres. Sharp stones cut into my knees. It was dark as dark. Everything seemed so noisy, my dress rustling against the earth, my heartbeats echoing in the night, my laboured breathing.

I was just under the bedroom window. I flattened my body to the ground as close as possible, just my right hand raised to hold the bottle.

Would I ever reach Iqbal? If I was caught I'd be put in the Tomb, too, with the scorpions and the snakes. I was sure there were snakes, whatever Salman said.

Finally, I bumped into Salman and Al`, who were sitting with their backs to the iron door.

'It took you long enough!'

'Where's Karim?'

We looked around.

'Karim!' we whispered. 'Karim!'

We saw his tall, skinny figure emerge from the shadows like a ghost. He was dressed in white, and was walking normally, slowly and calmly, with his hands in his pockets. All we needed was to hear him whistle. He looked as though he were walking in the sultan's gardens.

'You didn't really have to put on such a show, you know,' he said.

'Get down, fool!'

The heavy iron door was hard to open quietly. Its

hinges were all rusty and it was blocked by weeds. We tried to pull it open, and it hardly budged.

'Pull harder, come on!'

It moved a few centimetres, then a palm's width, and then we could smell the damp, heavy stench of the Tomb.

'Harder!'

The door turned on its hinges with a terrible squeak that seemed to cut the night in two.

'Quick!'

A light went on.

We stood absolutely still, paralysed like animals surprised by a hunter. I could feel my legs trembling, uncertain whether to stay or to flee.

'Run!' a voice shouted in my head. 'Run!'

Salman's hand blocked my arm.

'Don't move!' he hissed.

The bedroom window opened. A small square of light hit the courtyard. The mistress put her head out, looking first to one side, then to the other.

She'd see us, she couldn't *not* see us.

'I heard a noise, I tell you; I didn't dream it. It must be those damn children.'

We heard a faint grumble from inside the room.

'You! You wouldn't even hear a cannon! I'm going out to look,' she said.

Another grumble, this time longer and angrier.

The mistress leaned out as far as possible and

46

looked our way with her bleary eyes. We were there, only a few metres away, as visible as if we were in broad daylight, I swear. Visible like fireflies on a bush. I could feel her eyes on me.

But she didn't see us. She peered around some more, mumbled, closed the window with a bang, and turned out the light.

We waited. We waited for what seemed to be an eternity. Eventually my heartbeats slowed down, soothed by the sound of Hussain Khan's resumed snoring.

We went down the steep, slippery steps in single file. Our bodies were covered with perspiration. We had to move carefully as we tried to hold on to the slimy, mossy wall. We could hear the sound of metal beneath our feet: The metal ceiling of the Tomb was right below us. We stopped near the grating.

'Iqbal,' I called quietly. 'Iqbal!'

From his deep pockets, Karim brought out a box of matches. We could see Iqbal in the flickering light of the match. He forced himself up from the corner where he was crouching and came towards us. His lips were split from thirst and the flame of the match bothered his eyes.

The cistern that we called the Tomb was wide, but so low that anyone standing could touch the grating with the tips of his fingers. I passed the small bottle through the bars to Iqbal. He drank avidly and then poured the rest over his poor face.

His throat was too dry to let him talk to us, and although we had a million questions to ask him, we couldn't think of anything to say.

The sight of him suffering moved and confused me. And I remembered that this was only his first day in the Tomb. Salman was nervous. Karim behaved as if he was just passing by and had nothing to do with anything. Al` pushed his hand through the bars and took Iqbal's hand.

'Hold on,' he said. 'We're here now.'

'Yes,' I said, 'we'll come back every night.'

'I have to admit you're pretty brave,' said Salman.

'The hell we'll return,' said Karim. 'I'm not about to risk anything.'

'Thanks, friends,' croaked Iqbal. His voice was like a thin wire.

We went back every night.

Seven

Iqbal was released from the Tomb three days later. When we saw him walk across the courtyard on wobbly legs, blinded by the light, his arms covered with angry insect bites, we pitied him, but we were proud, too. We would have liked to cheer and applaud, but Hussain's grim eyes warned us to keep quiet. The master gave Iqbal a day and a night to rest, and we held back our curiosity and respected his fitful sleep. We took turns watching over him and soothing his pain by sponging him with cool water. We could see that Iqbal would recover quickly, thanks to our nightly visits, the food, the water, and those oranges that Al` had stolen from the garden for him.

'Brother,' said Salman one morning when Iqbal finally returned to work, 'you were really strong. Nobody has ever had the courage to do something like that to Hussain Khan. Do you realise how angry he still is about the carpet? But you were also foolish. What have you gained by destroying the carpet? Three days in the Tomb, that's all.'

'You all took risks, coming out at night to help me,' Iqbal replied. 'If the master had discovered you, what would you have got out of it?'

'What has that got to do with anything?' asked Salman. 'We did it for you.'

'Well,' said Iqbal, 'and I did it for you, in a certain sense, as well as for me.'

'What do you mean?' I asked.

'It means that this kind of life isn't right. We should return to our families; we shouldn't be chained to our looms and forced to work like slaves.'

'I'd like to go home, too,' I said, 'but we can't.'

'Why not?'

'Because . . . because . . . ,' burst in Salman, 'because the master is stronger than us. Because it's always been like this. Because nobody cares about us.'

'We'll find somebody to help us. Out there. There must be someone.'

'Out there? What's going on in your head?'

'I don't know,' said Iqbal.

'You got too much heat down in the Tomb, brother.' Salman shook his head. 'Everybody's too scared here.'

'That's not true.' Iqbal laughed. 'You're not afraid anymore. Neither are Fatima and little Ali.'

'I'm not afraid of anybody!' declared Ali, hiding behind my skirt.

'Even Karim is less frightened than before. Isn't that true?'

'Don't drag me into your dumb plans,' hissed Karim, 'and remember anyway, I'm not afraid of anything.'

'Not even Hussain?'

'I'm not scared of him,' Karim assured us. 'I respect him. It's different.'

'I think the others are less frightened, too,' Iqbal said.

'Back in line! Back in line!' yelled Karim, as he glimpsed the figure of the mistress crossing the courtyard.

For the next month things went as usual, at least on the surface. The days passed, all seemingly identical, the summer became less torrid, and every now and then we could see heat lightning in the night sky, reminding us that the rains were on their way. One of the older boys left with the master one evening, and we never saw him again. Perhaps Hussain had sold him to someone else, who knows? We were accustomed to this continuous change of faces around us, and we had even learned not to feel very sorry, or at least not to show it.

A new boy arrived in his place, tall and thin, with a

skinny back. You could count his ribs, each one. We immediately named him Twig. After only two days he hurt his hand, which Hussain had to bandage, crying out to heaven, lamenting the bad luck that had pushed him to make such a poor investment. Twig, armed with a broom, was set to cleaning the workshop, the courtyard, and occasionally the master's house. He went back and forth all day, with his arm in a sling, and he raised more dust than he eliminated.

That month an attack of dysentery obliged us to use the little place behind the curtain more often than we liked.

Nothing much out of the ordinary, it seemed.

But, now that I think about it, there *was* something different, though with all the work we had to do we didn't notice it at the time. We worked, as usual. We bore Hussain's harsh treatment, as usual. Every evening we watched the master take a rag and erase one of the marks on our personal slate and saw the marks remain the same, as usual. But still . . . the atmosphere inside the workshop had changed.

Nobody was working exactly as before. After the lunch break we reentered the workshop as slowly as possible, dragging our feet and mumbling. During the interminable afternoon hours our attention was easily distracted. We started talking and sometimes we even laughed. It took a few minutes for the shouts and threats of Hussain Khan to restore an apparent calm.

Twig wandered here and there, raising dust and increasing the general confusion.

One day a loom broke. It was used by Mohammed (the stammering boy from the mountains), and even though Hussein Khan was convinced it had been sabotaged, he had no proof, so he couldn't send Mohammed to the Tomb to rot for days. At another loom all the threads tangled, and it took hours to get it working again.

Iqbal was calm. The master had ordered him to begin the carpet again, and he was working carefully and precisely, nimbly and quickly, as though nothing had happened. Hussain Khan kept a constant eye on him. He walked grimly around the workshop, his hands behind his back, and every now and then he turned his head quickly to see what Iqbal was doing. Hussain seemed nervous – it was like *he* was frightened. And the more the carpet grew, the more nervous and irritable he became. But he didn't say a word to Iqbal, not a word.

'Hussain's afraid I'll destroy this rug, too,' said Iqbal, 'and it'd be a serious loss for him.'

'You won't do anything so stupid, will you?' I asked anxiously.

'Oh, no! I don't plan on anything like that,' he reassured me.

By now our evening get-togethers had become routine. We didn't even wait for the lights to go out in the master's house. As soon as Hussain locked the door and we heard his footsteps cross the courtyard, we left our beds and sat down in a circle. Twig, who was strange and funny, joined our group, and sometimes so did one or two of the others.

'We should all run away,' said Twig. 'Just think of Hussain's face! I can't stand him. He's almost worse than the master I had before. Let's become bandits and attack the trucks that come into the city.'

'Why the trucks?'

'Because they carry a lot of food.'

'Forget it,' said Mohammed. 'We should escape to the mountains. There the master would never be able to find us.'

'Yeah, and how did he find you?' Twig asked.

'Bad luck.'

We poured out our feelings. But we still feared that nothing would ever change for us. There was a precise rule among us: *Never* talk about the future. Not a single one of us dared to say 'next summer,' or 'in a year,' or 'when I'm grown up.' Oh yes, we talked about things we'd like to do, and we talked about the day our debt would be cancelled. We talked that hope into the ground. But nobody really believed it. It was a sort of litany, a way to feel good. Otherwise what was left to us?

Iqbal had been the first brave enough to say loud and clear that the debt is never cancelled. And he was the only one to talk concretely about the future.

One night while autumn rains were beating on the roof of the workshop, Iqbal and I sat together. We were always the last two to go to bed. We liked to stay up and talk.

'Fatima,' he said in a low voice, 'next spring you and I are going to go and fly a kite. Remember that, whatever happens.'

I didn't say anything. What was there to say? I only sensed he was about to do something rash and I wouldn't be able to stop him. He was so little, and yet he was so brave.

I said the only thing I could say: 'Please be careful, Iqbal.'

The next night, in the middle of a thunderstorm, Iqbal managed to squeeze out of the tight little window behind the filthy curtain at the back of the workshop. He ran through the neighbour's garden, climbed over a wall, and after crossing two more vegetable gardens, he reached the street and disappeared.

Eight

There was no news for two days. As soon as Hussain discovered Iqbal's escape he organised his friends and relatives, who climbed into their Toyota vans to search for the fugitive, swearing as they slid over the muddy roads.

We waited anxiously. We watched the courtyard gate. Hussain returned with a grim face late in the afternoon, his clothes soaked and his boots all muddied. He came into the workshop, where, heads down, we were all working at our looms.

'From now on,' he said, 'you'll all work an hour more a day. Every day.'

He put bars on the little window and Karim had to give him back the keys.

'You and I will talk about this later,' he said menacingly.

Karim was terrified.

Hussain went out again the next day, too, but he came back before the muezzin had called for midday prayers, then shut himself in the house.

As I worked I thought of Iqbal. Perhaps he had reached home and was embracing his parents. But the master would certainly go there to look and would threaten Iqbal's father and mother with prison if they didn't give their son back to him. Maybe he was still hidden somewhere in the city. Where would he sleep? What would he eat?

He's smart, I repeated to myself. *He'll manage.*

Then I remembered his promise: *In spring you and I will fly a kite.*

I wanted it to be true, but I tried not to delude myself.

I spoke to little Maria as if she were able to understand and answer back and comfort me.

'Do you know what a kite is, Maria? Have you ever played with one?'

Naturally she didn't answer.

'It's wonderful. You run and the kite rises higher and higher in the sky; sometimes it even touches the clouds, and it soars and veers with the wind. You have to be very careful, though. If you let go of the string, you lose the kite and after a while it floats away. It happened to me when I was too young and inexperienced. I was really sorry, and I cried for my lost kite. But at that moment, watching it fly higher and higher until it was swallowed up by the sky, it wasn't so awful. I thought, *Who knows where it's going?*

The morning of the third day we had just started working at our looms when a neighbour came running in. He and the master moved outside the doorway and the neighbour spoke very fast, gesturing with his hands. He looked scared.

Hussain and the mistress came into the workshop and told us to leave everything as it was. Then they pushed us across the courtyard, crying, 'Quickly! Quickly!' They pulled open the rusty iron door to the Tomb and made us bunch up on the steps.

'Stay there,' ordered Hussain. 'No one dare make a sound!'

Someone was knocking on the big outside door. I was trapped halfway down the stairs.

'What's going on?' I asked the child in front of me.

'I can't see very well,' someone whispered, 'but the master has gone to open . . . there are some people. It looks like . . . a policeman! There are two policemen . . . and Iqbal's with them!'

I elbowed my way up to the top step, where I put my eye to one of the rusty holes in the old door, and it was true. There were two policemen, fat and shiny with enormous black mustaches. They were wearing greasy, wrinkled uniforms, and their bellies hung over their belts, but they were policemen. Iqbal stood between them.

Hussain acted humble, bowing his head slightly and rubbing his hands together. Next to him the mistress twisted and tortured a corner of her apron.

I saw Iqbal raise his hand and point towards the workshop. The policemen walked slowly and calmly across the courtyard, skirting the puddles. When they reached the door they looked in, then talked to each other and asked Hussain something. Keeping his respectful attitude, he began to speak very fast, turning every now and then to ask the mistress to confirm what he was saying.

'What's happening?' someone from behind asked.

'I don't know. I can't hear what they're saying,' I answered, 'but I think Iqbal has accused the master.'

'Accused him?'

'You mean that now they'll put him in prison?'

'Quiet!'

Hussain became very animated, making broad gestures with his hands. The policemen looked bored. One of them took a look at an old-fashioned pocket watch. Hussain took Iqbal's hand and pulled, while Iqbal resisted, digging in his feet. Hussain gave his hair a rough caress, said something more to the policemen, handed Iqbal over to his wife, and gestured to her to take him into the house.

'No!' shouted Iqbal. 'No!' And then he said something more that was lost in a clap of thunder.

'What's happening?' the children behind me were asking. 'What's happening, Fatima?'

'I don't understand. They've given Iqbal back to Hussain.'

'You mean they're not going to arrest him?'

I could see Iqbal yelling and squirming as he tried to free himself from the mistress's grip, until they disappeared into the house.

It began to pour. The policemen were in a hurry. Behind me everyone was talking, but I hardly heard them. I couldn't believe my eyes.

Hussain stuck his hand into the wide band he wore around his waist and brought out a big wad of banknotes. He counted out a small pile and gave it to the first policeman, then he counted out another small pile and gave it to the second. They both nodded, satisfied. Then they pulled at their mustaches, put the money in their pockets, and went away in the rain.

Down on the steps to the Tomb we were all silent. Inside the house Iqbal kept yelling, but it was no use.

The mistress came to send us back to work. We didn't see Iqbal leave the house, but we heard all too well the bang of the grate of the Tomb as it closed over him.

The never-ending nightmare of our lives resumed.

We did all the ordinary things, but almost without realising it. Wake up, go to the bathroom (my little window was closed forever, but I didn't feel like jumping anymore anyhow), eat breakfast, work work work until it was time to go to bed. I cried, thinking of Iqbal locked down in the Tomb. I'd fall into a heavy sleep, then wake up suddenly to find that nothing was changed. Rainwater was dripping through holes in the roof. I was still a prisoner. Iqbal was still down in the Tomb. And this time we couldn't get out to help him.

I was afraid he would die.

Hussain Khan wasn't there. A few hours after the policemen came, he had left on a business trip. He had called Karim, in front of all of us, and said, 'When I get back, I'll measure everybody's work. Remember! You're the only one responsible for what they will have done.'

'Yes, master! Yes, master!' Karim obeyed.

'And as for that one down there . . .'

'Yes?'

'Leave him there.'

'Yes, master!'

Karim was terrified and he didn't give us a minute's rest, a single minute's distraction.

'You want to ruin me,' he repeated, 'but I won't let you. Get back to work! Work!'

I lost track of the time. How many days had passed? Four? Five? Six?

Iqbal was still down there.

I know he'll die.

At night we stopped meeting. Nobody wanted to. What good was it? Before Iqbal's arrival I had been resigned to my life. I couldn't even imagine a different one. Iqbal had sown the seeds of hope in all of us. Now the disappointment was too strong. He wouldn't be able to lead us anymore, and none of us had enough courage to rebel against Hussain.

He'll die, I thought, *and I'll be more alone than ever.*

Hussain Khan came back on a Friday, the holy day of rest for everyone – everyone, except us. He changed his clothes, greeted the neighbours who had come over to ask how his trip and his business had gone, then briefly took a look in at the workshop. He told Karim sternly that after lunch he would be measuring the work we had done. Then he went off to eat.

We weren't even allowed our usual break.

'You have to go on with your work,' Karim shouted. He was all sweaty and upset. 'Otherwise the master will blame me.'

I worked and tried not to pay attention to my hunger. The pungent aroma of spicy mutton wafted over from the master's house. I had eaten it two or three times. Back in my village the women prepared it for special occasions, like Choti Eid. It had to burn your tongue and throat, otherwise the men didn't appreciate it. The meat was fatty and tasty.

'Work.'

And perhaps they even had sweets, fritters with fresh, soft cheese, rolled in sugar. And cinnamon.

'Work.'

I was hungry. I was tired. I was desperate.

The master entered, picking at his teeth with a toothpick. We stopped our work and stood beside our looms. Hussain Khan rubbed his back, took out his tape measure and a piece of paper where he had written the length of our work before he left, and very calmly began his calculations. Then he took the slate and made his decisions: three marks gone, four marks gone, or no mark because the work hadn't been done well.

Nobody dared complain.

The master continued his counting, while Karim followed at his heels like a dog hoping for a bone. After the decision, we all bowed our heads in submission.

Salman, only one mark erased; Ali – 'It's a mess!' – not even one; and little Al` could hardly hold back his tears. Mohammed, three marks, and he whistled with relief. Hussain was at the back of the room. Now Maria . . .

Hussain Khan stopped short in front of little Maria's loom, and his eyes bulged. Karim didn't understand the terrifying look he received, but he whined in terror.

'And what is this?' roared Hussain Khan.

'I . . . I don't know . . . master . . . I . . . ,' stammered Karim.

We all went to have a look.

Maria always had the easiest patterns, carpets with simple geometric figures that didn't require any particular skill. She wasn't strong, and didn't even seem very smart, perhaps because of her deafness or whatever was wrong with her. Hussain Khan always said he kept her out of charity, but that wasn't true. She did her share of work.

We crowded in front of her loom. She had taken advantage of the fact that nobody ever paid much attention to her and that Karim behaved as though she didn't exist, and she had changed the carpet she was working on. In the middle of the carpet, instead of simple red and yellow stripes, there was now a picture.

It was of a kite.

A big, white kite, with long plumes tied to the tail. They seemed to be fluttering in the wind, and there was a thin string that hung from the kite and bits of white that were clouds. It was beautiful.

Maria was standing next to her work, looking even smaller, more delicate and defenseless than usual. Hussain Khan's mouth was wide open. He started to speak, but couldn't. He looked at Karim. He looked at all of us. He looked in the direction of the door for support from the mistress.

Now he's going to burst, he's so angry, I thought.

Hussain Khan uttered the only words he knew how to say, with a rattling voice.

'Into the Tomb! Into the Tomb you go, too!'

We gathered around him.

Maria was too weak and delicate to survive even a single day in the Tomb, and Hussain knew this as well as we did.

'Into the Tomb!' he repeated, but this time he didn't seem so sure of himself.

A voice screamed inside my head, *Do something! For the love of heaven, somebody do something!*

Hussain put out his hand to grab Maria.

From the corner of my eye, I saw Salman push his way to the front of the group.

'If you send her,' he said, trying to keep his voice firm, 'then send me, too.'

'What? What?'

'I said, punish me as well.'

Despite his pitted skin and his rough hands, Salman was beautiful at that moment.

'Well, what the hell,' said Mohammed, and he immediately began to stammer from the emotion, 'well then . . . s-s-s-s . . . s-s-s-s . . .'

'Go on!' they encouraged him from the back.

'S-S-S-Send me, too,' he concluded.

He looked around, satisfied as though he had made an important speech. He scratched his head and spat in the dirt like Karim.

By then we all had our hands up and were yelling, 'Send me! Send me, too!'

Even little Al` shouted from behind my skirt.

Hussain Khan was pale. He moved restlessly, unable to decide what to do. He tried to shout over our voices, but couldn't. You could see that he loathed us and that he would have liked to see us dead. But even he knew that wasn't possible.

And after a bit he gave up. We couldn't believe our eyes. Muttering various threats, Hussain Khan retreated. Karim slipped away with him.

Iqbal was back with us an hour later, after six days in the Tomb. He was exhausted, pale, and starving, but he was still alive.

Nine

That evening there was a large group around Iqbal's pallet.

'I reached the city just before dawn,' Iqbal began his story. 'The sky was grey. It was raining. There were great puddles everywhere, and I didn't know where to go. For a while I just wandered around. There are areas where the houses are very tall, so tall you can hardly see the tops of them, and areas where old decrepit houses are bunched together, but there was nobody about. It was too early. I finally reached a very long, wide street that led out of the city, and I thought *maybe this will lead me home, to the countryside, to my family.* I was planning to try somehow to sneak a ride on a truck or bus, when I realised that Hussain Khan would come to my parents' house and would force them to give me back to him. My mother would oppose it, but my father was a law-abiding man, and since he has this debt he wouldn't be able to say no. So I looked for the market square. It's enormous, did you know? You can't imagine how big it is. There are hundreds of wooden tables all lined up, and piles of crates and mattings where vendors put out their wares. Despite the rain they were already working. Mountains of fruit, truckloads of vegetables from the country, baskets and baskets of different-coloured spices, all covered with plastic. And the butcher stalls! Some butchers use sticky strips of paper to protect their meat from the flies, others just put it on the ground. They sell anything and everything there – old things, strange things, even crooked rusty nails.'

'Come on!'

'It's true, I'm telling you. And then there are stalls that are like real shops and they have big radios and tapes you can put inside to hear music.'

'I know,' said Karim with his usual superior air.

'And other tapes that they say show pictures.'

'I didn't know that,' admitted Karim.

'I walked around for hours. The market grew more and more crowded. I thought that if I stuck with the crowds it would be harder for Hussain Khan to find me. There were lots of things to see. I saw a juggler, and a snake charmer.'

'There's no such thing.'

'Yes there is!'

'And did the serpent sway to music?'

'Not really. But it came out of the basket. It was a big snake with a broad head and an evil eye, and the man held it in his hands.'

'Bare hands?'

'That's right. And there was food being sold everywhere. There were big pots of basmati rice and of chicken tandoori. It smelled so good. And I was hungry.'

'And so? What did you do?'

'I worked. They're there, too.'

'Who? Who's there?'

'Children. Working. They're the ones who unload the trucks and carry the crates, some so heavy they feel like they'll break your arms. You go to a merchant and say, 'Got any work for me?' And he says, 'Move that load and I'll give you a rupee.' That's what I did. But there were other children who didn't want me to do anything. They said, 'Who are you? Where do you come from? This is our turf. Any work here is ours. Get out of here.' I was afraid they would attract attention to me. After all, Hussain was out there looking for me. So I told them to leave me alone and I tried another area. Finally I found a butcher who let me unload a truck full of mutton hinds. He gave me a burlap sack to put over my head and shoulders to keep the blood off, which was lucky, because Hussain would never recognise me covered with burlap, and I knew he was after me. Once I even thought I glimpsed him in the crowd.'

'But what did you think you were going to do?'

'I didn't know. I thought I could hide a few days in the market and that I'd find something. I worked until the late afternoon, and I used the butcher's rupee for food. It had stopped raining and the sun was beginning to shine. I sat against a wall to rest. Two bigger boys came up to me. They were smoking and they had a strange way of speaking. 'Are you new?' they asked.

'"Yes," I replied.

'"Where do you come from?"

'"The country," I lied.

'"Looking for work? If you're quick, we have something you could do."'

'And what did they want you to do?'

'I never understood. But they had a knife, which they showed me. 'No thanks,' I told them, but they kept insisting I join them. I asked them where I could sleep, and they started to laugh.

'"Here. Wherever you want. Every counter becomes a hotel room, but be careful, new boy!"

'"Why?" I asked.

'"Just be careful!" they repeated.

'"I was scared. I felt lonely, and I didn't know what to do or where to go. I missed all of you, and I thought that maybe it had been dumb to run away. The market was emptying and night was coming. I felt so sad and homesick. I had escaped thinking that someone would help me and us, and there I was, all alone."

'So what did you do then?'

'I saw a bus, the big coloured kind with lots of lights and horns. Remember, Fatima, when I told you I wanted to ride one?'

'I remember.'

'So I got on and it took me around the city, until the conductor saw me and kicked me off. Then I took another, and another after that. I ended up in a place I didn't know. It was almost night. I was hungry again and the excitement of the bus ride was long gone. I fell asleep in a doorway, curled tight in a ball so I wouldn't feel the wind. In the morning the porter chased me away with a stick. I returned to the market, where I unloaded two truckloads of watermelons, always keeping an eye out for Hussain Khan. I thought I'd stay there for a few days, that the master would get tired of looking for me, so I'd be able to go home. But I wasn't sure. I was afraid I'd end up living there like a stray dog. Then that afternoon the men arrived.'

'What men?'

'There was a group of them. There were even some women. They put up a kind of platform and behind it a big banner and lots of signs. Of course, I didn't understand what was written on them. A large crowd formed immediately, and the police surrounded them. To help them, I thought. Then a man came onto the stage. I liked him the very minute I saw him. I thought, He must be a good man. He had a neat pointed beard and a clean white shirt. He began to speak into a microphone.'

'And what did he say?'

'He said . . . I remember well because I had never heard words like his before. He said, "We're from the Bonded Labour Liberation Front of Pakistan."'

'And what's that?'

'I don't know. But he said it was a crime, it was barbarous, to exploit children and make them work like slaves in carpet workshops or brick factories. He said that the masters are greedy and wicked.'

'Did he really say that?'

'I'm positive. And then he said that there's a law now in Pakistan: People who exploit children have to go to prison.'

'Yay! That's great! That's right! It's only fair!'

'Yes, but the majority of the people there didn't agree. The merchants insulted him and threw rotten vegetables at him. They yelled, 'Get out of here! Fool! Traitor!' The man with the white shirt managed to shout even louder. The crowd didn't intimidate him, and you should have seen how unruly the crowd was. The carpet sellers were the most ferocious. It looked like they wanted to attack the platform. They yelled that the man in the white shirt spoke only lies, all lies, but I thought, Here's someone who can help me and my friends. I tried to get closer to the platform to speak to him, but there were just too many people, and the platform was surrounded by policemen. So I thought, I'll talk to a policeman. They're here to help. That man says there's a law to protect children from masters. I said to the policeman nearest to me, 'That man's right about how masters exploit children workers. My friends and I are slaves of a carpet merchant.'

'"What are you doing here?" he asked.

'"I ran away."

'"And what's your master's name?"

'"Hussain Khan, sir."

'He looked around before saying, "Come with me."

'"Where?"

'"Don't be afraid. To the police station. We'll give you something to eat. And tomorrow morning we'll go see this Hussain."

'"Will you put him in jail?"

'"We'll know what to do."

'"At the police station they were very nice to me. They gave me a bowl of rice and they let me sleep on a cot in a cell. But I wasn't a prisoner. I could go away if I liked. At least, that's what they told me.

'You know what happened the next day. Hussain told them that we're workers, that he pays us regularly, that there aren't any chains. And they believed him.'

'They didn't believe him. They took money,' I explained. 'I saw them.'

We looked unhappily at one another. We were sitting

around Iqbal's pallet. He was still weak and very pale, and all the speaking was tiring him even more.

'If we can't trust the police, who can help us?' I asked, putting into words what everyone was fearing.

'The men from the Liberation Front,' answered Iqbal. 'They'll help us.'

'Maybe. But how can we find them?'

Iqbal smiled knowingly and pulled a piece of paper out of his pocket.

'What is it?'

'They were handing them out. There must be something written to tell us how to get to them.'

The paper passed from hand to hand. We touched it and looked at it, perplexed.

'Yeah, brother,' said Salman, 'maybe you're right. But you've forgotten something. No one here knows how to read.'

Silence fell.

Then a small voice spoke from behind the group, a voice we had never heard before. It was a strange voice. It sounded rusty.

'That's not true. I can read.'

With our mouths hanging open in surprise, we all turned around to look at Maria.

Ten

A new spring arrived.

The wind began to blow down from the mountains. At first it was cold, but then it softened and swept away the clouds, the smoke, and the dust of the city. The arrival of spring's breeze made us smile.

Strange flowers and weeds came up in the broken pavement of the courtyard. When we came out of the workshop at lunchtime, we were greeted with that good fresh-air scent. Mohammed lay in the sun and stammered with simple happiness. Karim lay in the sun and grumbled because he was afraid the master was mad at him. Twig was more sticklike than before, because his hand had healed and he had to work like the rest of us. Little Ali had grown like a mushroom over the winter, so he was no longer really our 'little' Ali.

And this was our big news of that spring day: Iqbal ran away again, and this time we knew he'd make it to freedom.

We had worked throughout the winter. Every night, by the light of pieces of candle Karim and Twig had managed to steal from the master's house, Maria taught us how to read. She wouldn't stand for any nonsense. Even reluctant Salman and lazy Karim were subject to her drive to teach. Our blackboard was the dirt floor, smoothed over with our hands. Our pencil was a pointed stick that we used to draw the letters of the alphabet, which we then had to repeat over and over.

'I don't understand anything,' Karim complained. He'd got confused after the first three letters. 'I'll never learn.'

'Be patient, you. You have to know how to read to ever be free,' insisted Maria, and she made him repeat everything again.

She taught us how to read, and we taught her how to speak again.

Maria's father was a schoolteacher in Faisalabad province. Her mother died when she was very young, and she had always played with dusty old illustrated books. She had learned to read almost by herself. Her father was almost as poor as the poor farmers who sporadically sent their sons to him.

'Your children mustn't be ignorant,' the teacher always explained, 'otherwise they'll end up as poor and downtrodden as you. Do you want that for them?'

'No, sir,' the farmers answered.

They did respect the schoolteacher and they did believe what he said. But times were what they were and children had to help out at home or in the fields, or in service to the master. There was no time for school.

'Go teach rich people's children,' the farmers suggested. 'Schooling is for the rich.'

But Maria's father never wanted to go to the rich. That is, until he finally had to ask for help from the village moneylender. And then he had to ask again. The second time he came home and didn't say another word, and the next morning some men came to take Maria away. Her father didn't even lift his head from the cot where he was lying. From that moment Maria stopped talking and reading. Now she was teaching herself again, as she taught us the strange symbols of the alphabet.

'What's your real name?' we asked her immediately.

'My name's Maria,' she answered slowly, bringing out the right words one by one. 'You named me. You're my family.'

A year had passed since Iqbal's arrival, and something had changed. Before we were a group of children facing the same sad fate, each of us just trying to survive. Now we were united, strong, friends and something more.

Maria's efforts were greatly rewarded one night, when we finally managed to decipher the handout Iqbal had brought back from his first escape. It seemed as if suddenly and miraculously, all those little marks we had drawn on the sand, those strange, incomprehensible pothooks, assumed meaning. We saw a sentence form on the paper, all by itself – I swear, we didn't do anything. It just came together, and it told us things.

I remember my heart beating like crazy. I couldn't believe my eyes! This, then, was reading. I looked at something dead and suddenly it came to life and it spoke to you, like a person.

We yelled 'Hooray!' and then we scurried back to our beds, because of course we had awakened the mistress.

We read the flyer out loud so many times that I can still remember what was written.

STOP THE EXPLOITATION OF CHILD LABOUR!!!

In Pakistan more than 700,000 children live like slaves, forced to work in the fields, in the brick-making kilns, in the carpet factories, for greedy and unscrupulous masters.

They are chained, beaten, tortured in every way.

They work from sunrise to sunset!

For their work, they sometimes receive one rupee a day – more often not even that.

Their masters get rich selling their prized carpets to foreign buyers.

The police know what's going on and don't intervene because of corruption.

But now there's a law in our country that makes these clandestine factories illegal.

Their owners should be arrested. Let's make them comply with the law!

Let's end this shameful and terrible crime, which exploits our children and

dishonours our country!

Our children have the right to be free children!

JOIN US!
FIGHT WITH US!
BONDED LABOUR LIBERATION FRONT OF PAKISTAN

And at the bottom of the flyer there was the address we had looked for, too. Now the problem was how to get there.

The brawl broke out without warning, while everyone was calmly enjoying the sunshine. When explaining the brawl to Hussain, some said that Mohammed, who was clumsy, had bumped into Salman, spilling Salman's bowl of lentil soup. Others said that Salman, who always tended to bully people, had started to tease Mohammed about his big feet, and the boy from the mountains had lost his temper.

Whatever the cause, within a minute they were really going at it, and before Karim could say 'Stop!' the fight had drawn in all the children. Some were on Salman's side, some were on Mohammed's, and some just enjoyed the opportunity of screaming and acting out. We girls played our part enthusiastically, running around the courtyard screeching like fools and raising dust.

The mistress dropped the big pot of soup she was carrying, spilling lentils every which way, and moved on her big, fat legs towards the house, calling her husband. Hussain Khan appeared at the door in his undershirt, his mouth and mustache greasy from his lunch.

'Stop it! Stop!' he shouted.

It took more than ten minutes to calm everyone down, and another ten minutes for the collective scolding, complete with the usual threats. Hussain sentenced Mohammed and Salman to a day in the Tomb, and dragged them down those familiar steps, while they continued to insult each other loudly. He then returned to his interrupted meal as the rest of us cleaned up the courtyard.

When we finished, Karim made us line up like so many little soldiers to go back into the workshop. After we started work, he slowly checked on everything. Then he went outside, thought for a moment, scratched his head, and spat in the dust two or three times. Taking his time, he strolled across the courtyard, hiking up his trousers as he walked, and knocked on the master's door. Then, to a shocked and angry Hussain Khan, he broke the news that one worker was missing.

Iqbal had taken advantage of the confusion to climb over the wall at the back of the courtyard. He took the path through the gardens and escaped again. He had just a small lead over his pursuers, but it would be enough.

Eleven

Iqbal came back the next day, and he wasn't alone. We recognised the man with the clean white shirt as the man Iqbal had seen giving a speech at the market for the Bonded Labour Liberation Front. His name was Eshan Khan. He was a tall, thin man who gave the impression of force and determination. His beard and his mustache were well groomed, and he was again wearing those immaculate white clothes. He had dedicated his life to the liberation of the child-slaves. He had been threatened, beaten, imprisoned; yet after each time, he had started afresh, driven by enthusiasm and perseverance.

He was stubborn, that's for sure, but above all, his faith in his ideas and his mission were unshakable.

We had never met an adult like him. Our parents were tired and unresisting. They lived in the same way their parents and grandparents had lived. They thought things would never change and that there was nothing to do to make them change.

Their masters took part of the harvest, the buffalo got sick, and the moneylenders took their lives and the lives of their children.

'This is the way it's always been,' they said.

Before meeting Iqbal, I thought that it was true, that being chained to a loom was part of the natural order. Eshan Khan opened my eyes even farther. It didn't matter that I didn't really understand everything he said. Eshan Khan became a second father for many of us, while never trying to take the place of our natural families. He was especially a father for Iqbal. It was inevitable. They were both reckless, determined, and convinced that the world needed changing.

When Eshan Khan and the two men from the Bonded Labour Liberation Front of Pakistan arrived at Hussain Khan's house, we realised that nothing could stop them. There was a policeman with them, too, but this one had a neat uniform and all kinds of things on his sleeves.

'He's an officer,' somebody said.

There was also a tall, thin man, who looked grim and severe. He said he was a magistrate.

And then there was Iqbal, with bright, gleaming eyes, jumping and making great signs with his arms.

'He did it!' we shouted. 'This time he really did it!'

Hussain threatened, argued, and begged. He twisted his hands and attempted to show the roll of banknotes he kept hidden in his sash. No one paid attention.

Iqbal took them into the workshop.

'Look at these children,' Eshan Khan said to the magistrate. 'Look at how thin they are. Look at their hands. Look at those cuts and blisters. And the chains.'

Then they crossed the courtyard and went down to the Tomb, reemerging with Salman and Mohammed, who squinted their eyes against the light, but who still managed to clown around and shout for victory.

The policemen took Hussain Khan away and the mistress shut herself up in the house, sobbing. They unlocked the chains, threw open the big front door of the factory, and said, 'Children, you're free. You can go now.'

Shyly, we all approached the door and looked up and down the street. A small curious crowd had gathered. Some people shouted. We went back in, bewildered.

'We don't know where to go,' someone said at last.

I felt lost, and so frightened.

'Let's take them to Headquarters,' Iqbal said to Eshan Khan.

They shuffled us into three big cars. As we drove away I managed to peek through the rear window: I saw Hussain's house, the workshop, the courtyard with the well, all becoming smaller and smaller in the faraway dust of the street. I had spent several years of my life there. Had I ever known another home?

Iqbal was crowded in next to me.

'Do you think we'll ever see it again?' I asked.

'No. Never,' he answered.

After a bend in the road, the workshop disappeared, but that little bathroom window of almonds, open sky, and hope would stay with me forever.

The headquarters of the Bonded Labour Liberation Front of Pakistan were in a big, old, two-story colonial house, with lovely pink paint peeling off its walls. There was a tall fence enclosing a small garden. The house looked onto a busy narrow street just behind the market. Despite its age and untidiness, it seemed beautiful and comfortable from the first moment. It felt like a true home, warm, free, and protective.

We entered a big room on the first floor, full of tables, wobbly chairs, and stacks of newspapers. We could see books and handouts piled here and there, plus signs and banners, and three stray dogs wandering in and out. Two ceiling fans did their ineffective best to cool the air, while telephones rang incessantly and men and women spoke loudly, waving their arms to emphasise what they said. When we passed through in single file, silence fell and they all applauded. We were so embarrassed that we could have sunk through the floor.

'This is the home of the Liberation Front,' Iqbal explained, 'and they're all volunteers. They're our friends. You mustn't be afraid.'

'Why are they clapping?'

'They're applauding us.'

'Us??'

On the second floor there were lots of rooms. We could see some women working in an enormous kitchen that smelled irresistible. The 'little place' for our needs was bigger than a town square, so clean, and with a mysterious gigantic tub. Three women ran to embrace us and touch us, chattering among themselves:

'Just look at these poor creatures . . .'

'How thin they are . . .'

'And their hands, take a look at their hands . . .'

'What about their feet? Look at their ankles . . . Such wounds . . .'

'And they're covered with lice . . .'

Before we could catch our breath, we learned what the big tub was for. It was filled with boiling-hot water, and despite our lively protests, one at a time we were caught, immersed, washed, scoured, scrubbed, brushed, and deloused. The women gave us clean clothes. Then they filled us with food and prepared beds in nearby rooms.

That evening at sunset, for the first time in my life, I enjoyed the feeling of a full stomach, a clean scent, and fresh bedding. The sounds from the street were closer than ever before: motors roaring, cars hooting, donkeys braying, voices exclaiming and laughing, a siren wailing, and from far away, a muezzin.

I'll never be able to get any rest, I thought, but then promptly fell asleep.

The next morning I woke up at sunrise, as usual, and looked around without realising where I was. My first thought was: *I'd better get to the loom. It's late and the master will punish me.*

I got up and dressed as fast as I could, then went out on the empty landing of the silent house and peeked down the stairs: no looms, no master, no work.

I sat down on the top stair and burst into tears. I hadn't cried in so long. I hadn't cried when I felt lonely and lost, a prisoner in Hussain's workshop. I hadn't cried when my hands bled after a long day's work. But now I couldn't stop sobbing. One of the women we had met the night before left her cooking and took me in her arms.

'Don't be frightened, little one,' she said. 'It's all over.'

But I wasn't crying from fear. It was something else.

Gradually everyone else woke up, feeling as dazed as me, judging from their expressions. We had breakfast and then scattered around the big room downstairs and the garden. We didn't know what to do.

The woman who had comforted me said, 'Children, play! The morning is yours.'

We broke up into small groups, feeling awkward. We hadn't played any games for years.

Eshan Khan came up to us in his white clothes, smiling. He gathered us around him and asked us the names of our villages, so the Front could trace our families.

'You'll be able to see your parents again,' he said.

Most of the children cheered for joy and crowded up to him, shouting names of strange, unknown places, but some stayed on the sidelines. Like Karim, who muttered, 'I don't have a family anymore. Where will I go?'

Little Maria sidled up close to me and whispered in my ear, 'I'm afraid they'll discover that my father's dead. I have only you. Where will you go, Fatima?'

Yes, where *would* I go? I wasn't so sure I could remember the name of my tiny village, and I had only the faintest memory of my mother, and some faded impressions of brothers and sisters. I couldn't even remember their names. Sometimes I felt I had only imagined them, that they had never really existed.

Iqbal approached me.

'You'll be going away, won't you?' I asked, remembering his determination to keep his memories, all the small details of his family life. He turned his face away, as if he didn't want to look me in the eye.

'Yes,' he muttered, 'I guess so.'

'You'll want to see your parents.'

'Yes,' he muttered again.

'And aren't you happy?'

He paused.

'I don't know,' he answered at last.

That was something I couldn't understand.

'You see,' he explained slowly, 'I really want to see my family, after all this time. I want to see my mother and my father, but I don't want to live their life.'

'Do you think they might sell you again?'

'That's not the reason,' he said. 'My parents, like yours, didn't sell me because they're bad. They had no choice. It was a terrible decision for them. No, it's not that. It's that I want to do something different.'

'What?'

His eyes fell on Eshan Khan.

'I don't know,' he murmured.

We stood there in silence, discouraged. Then Iqbal held out his hands to me and Maria.

'Let's go!' he cried.

'Where?'

'Let's go out. We mustn't be sad.'

'Go out? Can we?

'Of course we can. We're free!'

'What'll we do?' we asked together.

He smiled mysteriously.

'Eshan Khan has given me a present. And I have a

promise to keep with you.'

The city outside was new to us, strange and noisy. We couldn't stop staring. We climbed up the hill that dominates the city, until we reached a spot where there was only grass and stones and the midday sun. A kind of mist covered the city below us, but the spring air where we were was clear and clean and transparent.

'Don't look!' ordered Iqbal.

We covered our eyes, but as soon as I realised that Maria was peeking, I did, too. I saw Iqbal take a package from under his shirt. He unrolled something white and coloured on the grass. Then he began to run, yelling, 'Now you can look!' The kite was already high in the sky, dancing with the wind. It flew higher and higher. For hours we passed it from hand to hand, until a sideswipe of the wind broke the string and we saw it disappear as it aimed towards the sun.

We were sweating and breathless.

'We'll make another one,' we vowed.

In the late afternoon, as we returned down the hill, Iqbal said: 'I've decided. I'm going to stay with Eshan Khan, and both of you will, too.'

Twelve

That same evening, after dinner, Iqbal made a solemn declaration to the men and women who were meeting in the big downstairs room: 'I want to stay and help you free all the children who are slaves in Pakistan.'

Eshan Khan looked at him and smiled.

'That's not possible, Iqbal. You were very courageous when you rebelled and helped us rescue your companions, but you can't stay here with us. You belong to your family. What would your father and mother say if we didn't take you home to them?'

'What good will it do me to go home, if after a year or even sooner I'm a slave again? Or Maria, or Fatima? Or the others? How many children are out there working the way we were?'

'We don't know for sure. There are hundreds of clandestine carpet factories just in Lahore, and in the countryside there are the brick-making kilns. Up towards the mountains there are the mines. And then there are the farm slaves . . . tens of thousands of children, hundreds of thousands, maybe . . .'

'You want to free them,' said Iqbal. 'And, so do I.'

Maria and I watched, our mouths wide open, we were so impressed. Iqbal was talking like an adult.

'Think it over, Eshan,' one of the men said. 'The boy is clever and could be useful. You know how hard it is to get the magistrates to intervene. Iqbal could sneak in and talk to the children, who would trust him. He can find the proof we need. If it hadn't been for him, we would never have been able to stop Hussain Khan.'

Eshan Khan continued to shake his head.

'No. He'd have to learn so many things . . .'

'I'll learn,' Iqbal promised. 'I've already learned to read and write. Well . . . a little, anyway.'

'It's too dangerous. The carpet merchants and the kiln owners are very powerful. The moneylenders are influential. The police tend to protect them – you've already seen that. And the magistrates just look the other way. All of us here have been threatened and persecuted. No, we can't allow it.'

Iqbal stood up and drew himself to his tallest, which actually wasn't very tall. He looked immensely tall to us, though, as if he could touch the ceiling.

'I'm not afraid,' he said. 'I'm not afraid of anybody.'

They believed him.

Iqbal went home to visit his family. Ten days later Eshan Khan brought him back, and he spent the rest of the day closed up in his room. Towards evening he came out and said, 'My mother cried and my father was frightened for me, but now they understand my choice, and they approve. I've promised that I'll go back as often as I can, especially for our holidays, but I want to stay here, Fatima. I want to study. I want to learn everything I can. I want to be a famous lawyer and free all the children in Pakistan.'

'Good for you, Iqbal!' exclaimed Maria.

I said the same, but my voice trembled.

Iqbal did study. We all did. He also took part in the meetings of the Liberation Front, listening so carefully that his forehead would become wrinkled with the effort to understand.

Iqbal read books, too, sitting up at night by the light of a candle, spelling out every single word. He learned how to use a camera, and whenever he could, he talked to Eshan Khan. They talked for hours and hours.

They were made from the same mold, those two.

Over time our companions returned to their homes. Mohammed left to go back to his mountains, and he stammered out his goodbyes, trying to hide his feelings. Salman went home, too, and he said to Iqbal, 'Brother, I really liked what we did to Hussain, and I'd like to stay and do my share, but my folks need me.'

Our funny Twig left us, and little Al`, crying his eyes out. The others went, too.

Iqbal, Maria, and I remained, and Karim, who chose to do odd jobs around the house for his room and board.

Less than a month after we had been rescued, Iqbal managed to sneak into a carpet factory that was hidden in a damp cellar in the northern outskirts of Lahore. He found thirty-two children covered with scabies and wounds, so thin their ribs almost cut through their skin. He spoke to them. He showed them the scars on his hands to win their trust, and he took photos of the chains, the looms, the water seeping in. The place was raided three days later by some men from the Liberation Front, accompanied by a magistrate and policemen, who arrested the proprietor and freed the children.

All that night and throughout the next day Maria and I worked alongside Eshan Khan's wife and the other women, carrying pots of hot water back and forth for baths and making beds for the new arrivals.

Were they ever dirty! It was hard to believe that *we* were like that when we arrived.

Iqbal continued to take his declaration seriously. Over the next few months, he helped close eleven more factories. Almost two hundred children were liberated. They all passed through Headquarters, which at times looked like an orphanage! They were cared for and then sent back to their families. All the children told the same story, 'our' story. They came from isolated villages in the middle of the countryside; there was a bad harvest or an illness, and the families had to ask for loans from the moneylenders. Then the families had to bond their children to pay back the debt.

Iqbal wanted to do more.

'We have to hit the moneylenders,' Iqbal said. 'They're to blame for everything.'

By now he had taken his place in the meetings of the adults, speaking up with authority. He was tireless. The minute he finished one mission, he began another.

'We have to send them all to prison, every single one!' he would say.

Maria and I were uncomfortable when he was out scoping illegal factories. We worried and waited anxiously for his return.

One night he didn't come home and we were afraid something had happened to him. He returned the next morning with a black eye and a cut on his cheek.

'I found another workshop,' he said, 'but they caught me. They smashed the camera, too. Let's just wait a few days, then I'll go back.'

Eshan Khan was proud of him and treated him like

a son. And Maria and I were treated like daughters. We had everything we needed, but still I fretted sometimes. Iqbal's and my paths were going in different directions, and I felt that soon we would have to separate. I was also occupied by thoughts of my family. Sooner or later my relatives would be found. What would I do then?

But there were problems much more important than mine. Eshan Khan was worried. 'We have to be careful,' he said, 'because *they*, the moneylenders and the people who get rich by exploiting children, won't give in so easily. The more children we liberate, the more exploiters we accuse, the more they will try to silence us. That's what they're afraid of . . . our voice. They get rich and fatten where there's silence and ignorance.'

One evening I overheard Eshan Khan talking softly to his wife.

'It's Iqbal who worries me. By now they know him. They know that it's thanks to him that we can find them. He's so enthusiastic, but he's rash. We'll have to be more cautious.'

Soon there were two men on guard in the big downstairs room.

One night something woke us. We heard strange noises, then gunshots. Then there were shouts and the sound of running feet.

'What's happening?' we asked.

No one answered.

Out in the street some people shook their fists at us, and there were tough-looking men on the sidewalk in front of Headquarters. They would stand there for hours, watching us go in and out.

When I thought about Eshan Khan's *they*, I thought of Hussain Khan, but I also realised *they* had to be something even bigger and much worse.

Then came the episode in the market to reinforce my fears.

Even in a city as big and modern as Lahore, the outdoor market is the true centre of life and activity. Sooner or later during the day everybody passes through, perhaps to shop and meet friends, perhaps simply to look at people. Periodically the activists of the Liberation Front would go to the market, where they would build a little platform to speak from. Over the platform they hung a banner that said NO MORE CHILD LABOUR, and there were signs with slogans against bonded labour and slavery. The volunteers distributed handouts exactly like the one Iqbal had brought back to us at Hussain Khan's. The men gave short speeches, using a big trumpet-thing they called a megaphone.

A little crowd always gathered. The merchants, especially the richest ones, ridiculed and insulted the speakers. They even threw things at them. The majority of the audience listened passively. Only a few had enough nerve to show timid approval. These were usually farmers or labourers, usually people who understood what it meant to lose a child in that way. At least, that's what Iqbal *told* us, for Maria and I weren't allowed to go. They said it was too dangerous.

That day Iqbal spoke, too. He stood balanced precariously on a fruit crate, holding the heavy megaphone. Despite his shyness and embarrassment, despite the shouting, the whistling, and the racket of the onlookers, he managed to talk about his experience. He spoke about Hussain Khan and the carpet factory, about children chained to their looms. Then he named names. He shouted all the names he had heard during the meetings at Headquarters, the names of the great moneylenders, the names of rich, important, mysterious men who lived in luxury in the center of town, who traveled, who had business all over the world: Eshan Khan's *they*.

He called them flesh merchants, exploiters, vultures.

A riot broke out in the square. A small group tried to attack the platform, pushing, slapping. The police had to intervene, not very willingly.

They weren't in the square, of course. They don't go to the open-air market, but evidently they have lots of supporters.

The next morning, Eshan Khan came in with a pile of newspapers under his arm. There were articles in all of Lahore's papers, and also in a Karachi paper. Two of them even had printed photos of Iqbal, standing on the platform with that funny trumpet-thing in front of his mouth.

One of the papers called him 'the courageous child who had denounced his oppressors,' and another talked about the 'shameful exploitation of a child's innocence.'

'This is a good thing, isn't it, Father?' he asked Eshan Khan. 'You said that *they* keep getting stronger thanks to ignorance and silence. Well, this isn't silence.'

'Yes, Iqbal,' Eshan Khan said, 'this is good for our cause.'

But he didn't seem convinced. He looked worried.

I remember that period so well. Iqbal was happy, enthusiastic about everything, hungry and thirsty for anything new.

We were beginning to get used to our new life, to freedom. We could go out whenever we wanted . . . well, almost. Eshan Khan's wife kept a close eye on us. Once she gave us some money and we went to the movies. It was just like Karim said. We saw an Indian film that lasted four hours and I cried the whole time. Iqbal was nasty and wouldn't go see it a second time. We discovered television. We listened to strange music that came from far away – from America, they said.

Iqbal was full of plans for the future. He talked about them to Maria and me. He wasn't afraid of all the new things. I was, at least a little. Everything was happening so fast, or maybe I was afraid the happy dream would end, too fast.

One day a foreign person in strange clothes came to Headquarters. He said he was an American reporter. He interviewed Iqbal and Eshan Khan for two hours. A few days later an international correspondent came.

'When people abroad know about our cause, they'll help us and we'll be safer,' said Eshan Khan.

One night we were awakened by a loud explosion. We could hear screams and see flames rising up to the windows on the second floor. We tried to go downstairs but Eshan Khan stopped us.

'You stay here!' he roared.

Someone had thrown two incendiary bombs against Headquarters. A man was injured and had to go to the hospital. *They* had sent a warning.

Thirteen

One day in the fall, the Liberation Front heard about an illegal brick factory and went to investigate. Iqbal went with them, and told us about it the next day.

'We travelled for more than an hour in the dark. The night was cold, so we took cover under the tarp in the back of the pickup truck. We must have looked like little babies under a blanket.'

'I wish I had seen you!'

'I felt like laughing, but something stopped me. Everybody felt strained. They were very serious and nervous. Nobody was about to laugh. Eshan Khan had warned us before we left. You both heard him. 'Be careful! Be careful! This time it'll be much more difficult than usual.' In fact, we had never done anything like it before. After awhile we turned off the main road onto a dirt track full of potholes. I haven't the slightest idea where we were. There was only darkness, silence, and that freezing wind that bit at our noses.

'We came in sight of the kiln just before dawn. There was a large level clearing, all stones and mud. There wasn't a tree to be seen, not even a blade of grass. The kiln was ugly; in the early light it looked like a hill of bricks with a tall thick chimney. People were already working, because they can produce the most bricks in the early hours. Later on the sun and the heat and the fatigue take all the strength from their arms. When we arrived nobody even paused to look up at us. You should have seen them. They were scattered throughout the clearing, almost like ghosts. Each family has its own hole, where the boys use a little hoe to dig because the clay is hard. They mix the clay with water to make little round loaves of mud. The girls fetch water from the well, which is almost a kilometre away. They go back and forth carrying big plastic twenty-litre jugs. The boys throw the clay loaves to their mothers, who knead them like bread and then throw them to the fathers. They put each one into a wooden mold, scrape away the excess, and then overturn it onto the ground, where it will dry in the sun. The bricks are in long rows that cross the clearing. The rows get longer every minute, like the tail of a snake.'

'So whole families work there.'

'They have to. They get paid by the piece. They

102

have to make twelve hundred bricks to earn a hundred rupees.'

'A hundred rupees! That's a lot of money.'

'That's what I thought, too. But listen. We got out of the trucks and approached a family, and Eshan Khan told them who we were and what we were there for. The man didn't even lift his head. He was crouched on the ground, and every thirty seconds he turned out a brick. He was dirty. His hair and beard were full of clay. Eshan Khan insisted. The man never looked up or stopped working. He just murmured, 'For the love of God, brother, get out of here.' I swear it made me want to cry. It's always terrible to see a little child working in inhuman conditions. We know what it's like. But this was worse. Because this time it was a man. A grown-up. A father. And . . . and . . . I don't know . . .'

'What?'

'He didn't seem like a man anymore. He didn't have anything anymore. Like all of them. There they were, in the early morning light, crawling along their rows of bricks. Now I know why Salman refused to talk about work in the brick factory.

'I moved away from the others and got closer to the hole and I spoke to the children, but at first they didn't want to answer me, like their father. Then the eldest, about my age, started to talk, all the time digging with his hoe and pouring on water. He was covered with mud from his head to his heels.'

'What did he tell you?'

'That there were six of them in the family, and that on lucky days they even managed to make fifteen hundred bricks. If the clay wasn't too hard. If there was water in the well. If only a few bricks broke in the heat of the sun, because broken bricks don't count. That on some days they earned a hundred twenty rupees, but that wasn't enough.'

'Why not?'

'Because they had to pay rent for the hut they lived in. The boy explained this to me. He pointed to a low, narrow building next to the kiln, and told me that each family has a hut, three metres by three, with a small cooking stove, some cots, and a window without glass. They have to pay the master for everything. They have to pay for the coal they burn and the food they eat. Everything costs a lot. Once they've bought grain for bread and some lentils and onions, a small bottle of oil and some vegetables, nothing is left of their day's earnings. The family had an enormous debt, but they weren't able to pay back a single rupee. The boy told me that he'll inherit the debt from his father, and his children will inherit it from him. Then he said, "Go away. The *munshi* – the director – will arrive in a few minutes, and he doesn't like to see people here."'

'So what did you say, Iqbal?'

'I didn't know what to say. Then I caught a glimpse of their feet, his and his brothers'. I looked away

104

quickly, but the youngest, who was about five years old, noticed and started to laugh. 'Look!' he said. The soles of his feet had a two-inch, black callus, all cracked. When the kiln starts, they have to climb on top with baskets of coal and pour it into the hole in the middle to get the fire going.

'"The kiln is like a dragon," the boy said. "It eats and eats but it's never satisfied. You should hear how it grumbles and then spits flames."

'"And doesn't it burn you?" I asked.

'"Of course it burns!" he answered, and I couldn't think of anything else to say to him.'

I had never seen Iqbal so depressed. All the men had come back grim and discouraged that day, even Eshan Khan, who was always optimistic and ready to smile.

'Then what happened?' I asked him, even if I already knew, because word had spread as soon as they got back.

'The *munshi* arrived in a big car. When he saw us talking to the workers he got very angry. He yelled at us to go away. Eshan Khan explained who we were and told him that we had the right to speak to these people, that they were free. The *munshi* just yelled louder. That always happens, you know that, so we weren't worried. Then the *munshi* ran into a green iron hut. It was his office, the only building with electric light. We could see the wires. We thought that maybe he was going to phone somebody, his partners or maybe the police.

105

Eshan Khan told us to stick together, that they couldn't do anything to us. Then the *munshi* came out of the hut with something dark in his hand, and he stretched his arm out towards us. He had a gun. We heard the first shot while we were scattering through the clearing, while we slid in the mud, while we looked for a way out of there. He shot and shot and screamed insults at us, and I didn't think he'd ever stop. He was shooting to kill, and it's a miracle that nobody got hurt. We got back in the vans and trucks and drove away fast. It's the first time that's ever happened.'

Later on, towards evening, Iqbal and I were waiting to be called to dinner. The usual sounds of the street came in through the windows.

'This hasn't changed a thing, Iqbal,' I said.

'I know. We'll keep on working.'

There was something else he wanted to say to me. He lowered his voice to a whisper. A truck was passing down in the street, and I could barely hear him.

'I was scared, Fatima. But please. Please. Don't tell anybody.'

I put out my hand to touch his shoulder, but then I pulled it back. I felt shy.

'Dinnertime!' Eshan Khan's wife was calling.

'Don't worry,' I said very softly, 'I won't tell anyone.'

That was one of our last long conversations, because a few weeks later, Iqbal departed, and I went home.

I wish I had been brave enough to actually touch him.

fourteen

One dull, rainy day at the beginning of November, Eshan Khan called Iqbal and me into his personal office. We entered the small, whitewashed room, which was almost empty and very neat. It stood in complete contrast to the rest of the house, which was full of papers, signs, colour, and confusion. Here was a desk under neat piles of papers, a telephone, a chair that didn't look very comfortable, makings for tea, and a strong smell of tobacco. Eshan Khan was walking impatiently back and forth, his eyes shining. He was holding a big brightly coloured ball. We had already seen it a few times and we thought, *Oh, no! Another geography lesson.*

Eshan Khan spun the ball and showed us a big area coloured yellow. 'This is the United States,' he said. 'It's a big and important country.'

'I know,' said Iqbal, hoping to avoid a lesson. 'It's the place where they make the songs.'

'Where there's Hollywood and the movie stars,' I said to help him.

Ignoring our show of knowledge of American culture, Eshan Khan pointed to a small black spot on the edge of an enormous sea.

'This city is Boston,' he continued. 'Every year a company called Reebok awards a prize that's called 'Youth in Action.' It's given to a young person who has done something of merit in any country in the world.'

'I know Reebok,' insisted Iqbal. 'They make shoes. I've wanted a pair for months, but they're too expensive.'

'The prize is fifteen thousand dollars.'

'How many rupees is that?' I asked.

'More than we can imagine. This year the prize has been awarded to Iqbal.'

Silence.

'To me?' Iqbal asked, confused.

'Yes, and do you know what it means? It means that now you're known all over the world and so is our fight against child labour. It means that from now on, *they* will have to be careful before they try to touch us in any way. It's a victory, Iqbal, and it's all thanks to you. You and I will go to Boston to receive the prize. But first' – Eshan Khan turned the globe – 'we'll stop here.'

He pointed to another country.

'This is Sweden,' he said.

'And what's that?'

'A country where it's very cold. It's in Europe. There's going to be an international conference on labour problems. People will be coming from all over the world. They want to hear you speak.'

'Me?'

We were astonished. It was like a dream. It was difficult for us to believe that others, in that faraway and unknown place called the world, knew about us and our suffering. We were nobodies, wretches who just a year before had been working at our looms, some of us chained to them. And all those people wanted to listen to Iqbal!

'There's more,' said Eshan Khan. 'A university near Boston has given you a scholarship. It means you'll be able to get a degree. Didn't you say you want to become a lawyer?'

Iqbal nodded without speaking.

'But . . . that means . . . we'll have to go . . .'

'We'll be away almost a month,' said Eshan Khan. 'Just wait. You'll like travelling. You'll see so many new things. When we get back you'll begin your studies, and later on you can go visit your family. You must be happy.'

'I am happy,' answered Iqbal, 'but I want to stay here, with you and Fatima and Maria. I want to free more children.'

'You'll still be helping us. You're important. But later on, if you become a good lawyer, you'll be even more useful.

'Today there's good news for Fatima, too. We've found your village, and your family. You'll be going home.'

My heart jumped. Home! I could hardly remember it. And my mother? And my brothers and sisters?

Suddenly I wanted to cry, but I felt silly. Why should I want to cry at good news? I was about to return home – free! Iqbal was going to receive a rightful reward for what he had done. Everything was going well. Whoever could have foreseen all this when we were working like slaves for Hussain?

I did cry, and it was because I was so happy.

The next two weeks just flew by. The big pink house boiled over with activity, everyone running from one end to the other, getting things ready for the journey. Reporters from Pakistan and abroad wanted to know about the prize. The garden was always full of people. For me, every sunset held sadness and hope.

How much longer before Iqbal left? Nine days.

I have memories of Eshan Khan talking into three microphones. Of a stranger wandering around, taking photos of all of us. I should have made him give me one – at least I'd have that now. I remember the women kneeling with pins in their mouths, fitting the

Western-style suit that Iqbal would wear at the ceremony. It had a jacket, trousers, and a waistcoat, all in a heavy dark blue material. It would be cold where he was going.

One day I came upon Iqbal all alone in the middle of an empty room, while he was practising the speech he would give in Sweden and in Boston. He tripped over every sixth word, and then said, 'Come on, Fatima, help me!' so I took the written speech and, reading a little slowly, gave him the right cues.

'. . . *Every day in Pakistan seven million children get up in the dark before dawn. They work all day, through evening. They make rugs, they make bricks, they work the fields, they go down into the mines. They don't play or run or shout. They never laugh. They're slaves and they wear chains on their feet . . .*

'. . . *So long as there's a child in this world who is deprived of his childhood, a child who is beaten, violated, or exploited, nobody can say:* It's not my business. *That's not true. It's your business, too. And it's not true that there's no hope. Look at me. I had hope. You, ladies and gentlemen, you must have courage . . .*'

How much longer before he left? Six days.

In a rare afternoon of quiet, Eshan Khan's wife took me in her arms and said, 'Poor little girl.' Then she explained that my mother was dead and that now my brother Ahmed was the head of the family. He was impatient to see me, because he had plans to go far away, to try his luck in Europe. He wanted to take me and my little brother Hasam with him.

I was going home to my family after Iqbal's departure. Maria promised to keep me informed about everything that went on. Before I left for a foreign country, I'd come back to Headquarters to say goodbye.

The last night Iqbal and I were together, we got up and met in the big room, where we talked and talked, just as we used to in Hussain's workshop.

At dawn the next day they let me ride in the car with Iqbal and Eshan Khan to the airport. Iqbal and I sat in back. From a terrace I watched them board the plane. They waved, from so far away.

With a loud roar the plane took off and flew higher and higher through the sky.

Iqbal had taken the biggest kite.

My heart was beating very fast. Something was wringing my heart and soul. The plane disappeared beyond the horizon.

I wonder what America's like, I thought.

A few days later I was taken home. I can still remember the long journey in the Toyota van as it bumped over all the holes in the road. I can remember the countryside, part green, part grey and flooded. I can remember the working men and the beasts. I remember the muddy dirt roads.

Every time I saw a group of huts, I thought, *Is this my village?*

I couldn't trust my memory, and I was confused.

The driver was kind and pleasant. He talked and talked to distract me, as though he knew what I was feeling. Part of me wanted to go home, part of me was sorry.

We arrived. My brother Ahmed was now a man. Hasam, the youngest, was taller than me. Slowly, gradually, I began to recognise objects that were once familiar to me. I found my way to the well instinctively. I had gone there so many times in the past, trying to balance a jug on my head.

Even the buffalo looked the same, only a little older.

I cleaned, I cooked, I helped in the fields, just like my mother had done. I didn't know anything about my brother's plans and I wasn't interested.

The days and weeks passed. In the country they seemed much longer.

I finally received a letter from Maria. I ran to read it outside.

She wrote, *'Here everything's going well.'* She said that Eshan Khan had telephoned, once from Sweden, twice from America. Maria had spoken to Iqbal, who was fine. He told her all about the speech he had given in a big city called Stockholm. He hadn't tripped up once. In fact, all those well-dressed people had stood up and applauded him.

They had welcomed him warmly in America, too. In Boston, everybody wanted to meet him, and when they gave him his prize some ladies cried. The only thing he complained about was his new shoes. They hurt his feet. He sent his love to me. They were about to return. School would resume, and later on Iqbal would go to visit his family for Easter. He hoped I was well and wanted to know what my village was like. She would write again. *'Kisses, Maria.'*

There was a folded article from an American newspaper in the envelope. Naturally I couldn't read it, but in several places I could see the name 'Iqbal,' and there was also a photograph of him. I looked at it for a long time, even if it was dark and smudgy.

Time passed. With a piece of chalk I made marks on the wall in a corner, to keep count. Two weeks, a month, three, then four. Winter passed, and the spring rains began. I stopped counting. The lame man who came to distribute and collect mail every ten days wasn't to be seen.

'We'll be leaving soon,' my brother Ahmed said.

When I finished my work I would sit in the doorway and look out towards the path that led to the village. *They've forgotten me*, I thought.

My mind went back to the kites, to Iqbal standing tall next to the carpet he had cut, to the night we crawled to the Tomb to help him, to the afternoon in Lahore when we went to the movies. I thought that I didn't want to go to a foreign country, far away and ugly.

Two days before we were supposed to leave for Europe, I saw the lame man in the distance. He was struggling along the muddy paths. His bag was slung on his shoulder and his stick sank five inches into the mud at each step.

The light was ugly that day, livid and nasty. The clouds lay low on the horizon and everything looked spotted and black. I watched him for half an hour, as he came along so very slowly. Before he reached me with the letter my eyes had started crying.

fifteen

Dear Fatima, my friend, beloved sister,

How I wish you were near me these days, so I could talk to you and cry with your arms around me. Do you remember how many times I've done so in the past? And you were always able to find the best way to console me and to protect me. If you could only do it once more! If we could only share our common grief! If only I could be the one to find the right words!

I know I haven't written for a long time. Maybe you thought I had forgotten you, that my affection had vanished like the mist on morning fields. My silence was because I didn't want to be the one to break the news to you. Even now my hand trembles and my tears fall. Forgive my cowardice, Fatima. I know you mustn't learn from others – who knows what they might say? I'll tell you.

At Easter, the Christian festival, Iqbal went home to his village. He went there to visit his family and celebrate. He *was supposed to spend a month with his parents, and then return to us, to continue his work. He said that he had made a promise in front of all those people in America, and that he meant to keep it.*

You know what he was like.

They say that the village welcomed him joyfully, like a hero. Everyone knew what he had done and they admired and respected him. Everybody in the village visited his home, brought him presents, and asked if it was true that he had been in a plane.

They say that after two days he was tired of all this attention and began avoiding people. He preferred to get up at dawn and go out into the fields with his father instead. In the afternoons, he rode an old bicycle with his two younger cousins, or together they flew kites. He was happy and serene and full of plans for the future.

They say that Easter Sunday was a lovely day, full of sunshine and light. Iqbal went to his church and then went around to visit relatives. There was a big feast, with singing and dancing, and there was even meat to eat, and all kinds of sweets, and Iqbal ate enough **laddu** *to cause a stomachache. Then, while the adults were talking among themselves, the children scattered off to play, and their voices could be heard in the distance.*

They say that around three that afternoon – when the sun was beginning to go down – a car appeared just where the road turns in towards the village, raising a cloud of dust. Nobody recognised it. It was a big black car, covered with mud. It looked as though it was driving by itself, and it whipped up the gravel with its enormous wheels as it passed.

Some people say that at that precise moment a sudden thunderstorm broke, and raindrops the size of large coins hit the ground and the thunder shook the roofs of the houses. Others say that the thunderstorm broke later, towards evening.

The black car drove slowly through the village and then turned into a narrow lane that leads down to the rice paddies. The pouring rain and the water in the rice paddies merged as one.

They say that Iqbal was riding up the lane, standing so that he could pedal better, with his wet hair in his eyes and his T-shirt flapping in the wind.

Nobody knows what happened, Fatima, my sister. A man has murmured that through the curtain of falling rain he saw Iqbal pass close to the car. The window came down a little, and there were three, four, maybe five flashes. Before anyone could get the men together and run to help, the car had disappeared. Iqbal's body was there, fallen in the lane, and the water under him was stained red, but even the red water disappeared soon. The rain washed it away. This is what they have told me.

But listen, Fatima. I know it's not true.

At first I thought I had become mute again. I had closed up inside. I kept saying to myself, 'It's not true, you know

118

what people are like, how they imagine things, how rumours persist.' Everyone else was convinced the news was true, even Eshan Khan and his wife. I was the only one who didn't believe it.

Then, one afternoon two weeks ago, there was a knock on the garden door. It was a boy, dirty and with bruises from chains around his ankles. He told us he had been working in a carpet factory, that he had run away and come to us so that we would help arrest his master and free the other children.

And then, do you want to know what he said?

'I'm not afraid.'

I looked at him carefully, Fatima. It was Iqbal. I swear, he was identical! The same voice, the same eyes.

Three days later another boy appeared. And then at the market a boy rebelled against his master, one of the richest merchants.

They were Iqbal, too.

Try not to be sad, Fatima. He changed our lives and will be with us forever. I told Eshan Khan that I'll be the one to study and go to university. I'll be a lawyer, and I'll fight to free all the slaves in Pakistan and all over the world. And for the first time in my life, I'm not afraid either.

My sister, I don't know where you're going, or how I'll be able to communicate with you, or even if we'll meet again. I just beg of you, don't forget. Tell somebody our story. Tell everybody our story. So that the memory will not be lost.

That's the only way to keep Iqbal at our sides forever.

Your sister,

Maria

Epilogue

Iqbal Masih was murdered on Easter Sunday in 1995, in Muritke, a village some thirty kilometres from Lahore, Pakistan. He was about thirteen.

His murderers have never been discovered.

'He was killed by the Carpet Mafia,' Eshan Khan declared.

Iqbal's name has become the symbol of the battle to liberate millions of children throughout the world from violence and slavery.

For further reading on Iqbal Masih and child labour laws, see the following sources:

Iqbal Masih
http://www.childrensworld.org/engiqbal/index.asp

http://www.freethechildren.org/campaigns/cl_realstories_iqbal.html

Kuklin, Susan. *Iqbal Masih and the Crusaders Against Child Slavery.*
New York: Henry Holt & Company, 1998.

Children's rights
A Life Like Mine: How Children Live Around the World. New York:
DK Publishers, 2002.

Castle, Caroline. *For Every Child: The UN Convention on the
Rights of the Child.* New York: Phyllis Fogelman Books/Penguin
Putnam Books for Young Readers, 2001.

Child labour
Campbell, Susan Bartoletti. *Kids On Strike!* Boston: Houghton
Mifflin, 1999.

Freedman, Russell. *Kids at Work: Lewis Hine and the Crusade
Against Child Labour.* New York: Clarion Books, 1994.

Mofford, Juliet H. (ed.). *Child Labour in America* (Perspectives on
History Series). New York: Discovery Enterprises Limited, 1997.